Children Under Foot

IRENE LaFETRA

Salt of the Earth Press
Springbrook, Wisconsin

Cover photograph copyright © Molly Bob
Book design by River Gathering Books

Published by Salt of the Earth Press, Springbrook, Wisconsin.
Printed in the USA
Salt of the Earth Press web address: www.saltpress.com

This book is for my children,
because even when it's been crazy and hectic
and we were barely scraping by,
I loved every minute being their Mama.

Chapter One

The pungent aroma of sautéing onions filled the small cottage but it was not strong enough to overpower an underlying odor of backed-up plumbing. Sali stood at the door, one hip thrust out to support the baby straddling her, and tried to maintain a look of intelligent interest as the stranger's nostrils flared in a disgusted recognition of the smell.

"Uh, as I was saying, Mrs...., well, as I was saying, I just moved in next door and your children have absconded with the boxes I left on my back porch." The man was tall, a little older than her 32 years, about forty or so, and too thin in the way that musicians and earnest teachers often are. Beneath a high forehead, his dark brows were knotted in concern. Black hair, shaggy though neatly combed, fell over his forehead giving him a boyish look. Using one long finger he pushed his wire rimmed glasses up a little higher on his straight nose and peered at her.

"Oh, dear. You know how children are. They probably made a fort out of them. But you did say you were moving in so you won't be needing them, right?" Sali tried smiling as though she were oblivious to the man's irritation.

"Madam, the boxes had not been unpacked yet!" he

said forcefully and Sali saw that the problem would not be obliterated easily. Her stomach twisted a little as her mind frantically tried to recall any unusual items turning up around the house. Because of her concentration she wasn't aware of the dark scrutiny her neighbor gave her. Draped all over in a baggy T-shirt and drawstring shorts and tall for a woman at five feet nine inches, the woman was a little round in the hip and calf, not to mention the chest, with arms that could knock a sumo wrestler to his knees. She appeared anything but delicate. She must get her muscles from hoisting that huge baby about, he remarked to himself, wondering why the child couldn't walk or stand or even sit but must be carried about ponderously like some ancient potentate. Her dark brown hair curled in wild disarray halfway down her back and hadn't seen a stylist in some time, he would guess. Her face was scrubbed clean except for that smear of chocolate on her cheek, oh, please let it be chocolate, although the odor...

"Crap!" Sali spat out startling the gentleman. "I am so sorry! *Kids!*" Her voice was enough to wake the dead and nearly knocked Sam Thompson down the steps, such was the shock of it. Green eyes narrowing in anger she burst into a yell. "Albert, William, Stephanie, Bridget, Josephine! Here! Now!"

Sam fully expected there to be a stampede of feet rushing to her summons but the house stayed ominously quiet and Sali shook her head. "I'll find them and I'll find whatever is yours. I am sorry. They really are just kids and kids can be, well, they can be horrible at times, but really they are good kids... and, I'm sorry. But I guess I already said that." Her voice wound down and her eyes shifted to the doorjamb in avoidance of his amazed gaze.

"Are they all yours?" he asked in shock. He had assumed that a couple of kids and their friends were to blame, never dreaming that he was moving in next door to a day care. Didn't this woman know that it was out of vogue, not to mention irresponsible to fill her house beyond capacity with children she obviously was ill equipped to care for? If that plumbing odor was any indication, Sam didn't even want to imagine what the house actually looked like.

"Yes, they are all mine," she said in a tight voice. The baby took one chubby fist out of its mouth and patted Sali's cheek in a parody of comfort leaving behind a glistening spot of saliva that she was oblivious to. One thatch of sandy brown hair stood up stiffly from the top of his little round head. Her eyes flashed sparks and her mother's heart became fierce. "They are all mine, Mr....?"

He dragged his fascinated eyes away from the baby slobber on her cheek, mentally shaking himself, "oh, Thompson. Sam Thompson. Let's start over. Hi, neighbor. I'm Sam Thompson. And you are?"

Sali managed to restrain her Irish urge for justice and thrust out her free hand, "I'm Sali Kelley. Nice to make your acquaintance." Just as Sam's hand clasped hers he was horrified to recognize that the odor was not coming from inside the house but was, in fact, coming from the baby and, if he wasn't mistaken, the hand he now held in his had some remnant of the baby's business on it from juggling the diaper clad bottom.

"Well, Sali," he said as he tried to unobtrusively wipe his hand along the sides of his jeans, "I've just moved in and your children may have thought that some of my unpacked boxes were to be discarded."

"I am so sorry, Sam," Sali said in imitation of his conciliatory tone, "I will question them all and get right to the bottom of it." She shifted the baby to her other hip, suddenly noticing all at once that the onions were no longer sautéing but rather burning and the baby's diaper seemed to be leaking. She spun on her heel without a word and in several strides had disappeared into the dark reaches of the small house. Sam, feeling a little awkward, but determined to have his things returned, followed close behind.

The interior was shadowy with curtains drawn against the strong California sunshine but there was enough light so that Sam got an impression of small spaces, crowded with furniture, and cluttered with the assorted belongings of numerous children.

Sali marched through a doorway that Sam recognized as the kitchen and quickly turned a knob on the stove. She rotated smartly on one heel so quickly she almost ran into him, but rather than move to the side just barreled through into a hallway where she plopped the baby down on a bed in a room that seemed filled with beds. Sam was awestruck; first by her fast assessment of what was important - turn the stove off and then change the baby, although he wasn't sure he would have been able to hold onto the smelly child any longer - and second that such a small room could hold so many beds. There was one against the wall near the door and two more stacked bunk style on the far end. They each had a bedroll upon them, and a pillow and one stuffed animal, though one of the stuffed animals looked suspiciously and ferociously like Godzilla. After he had done an assessment of the room he returned his eyes to her and the baby.

Sali had expertly removed the dirty diaper, rolled it neatly into a sausage, refastened the tapes to hold it in that sausage, whipped open a box of wipes and somehow extricated several all while holding the wriggling, squirming baby still to keep from creating a greater mess. In no time the baby was clean, a fresh diaper fastened across the pink bottom, a boy Sam had noticed, and Sali was standing in front of him holding out the child. "Huh, what do you want me to do with him?" Sam asked in horror.

"Just hold him a minute, would you, please, so I can wash myself up. He seemed to have sprung a leak." She waved one odiferous arm under his nose while pushing the small arms against his neck. The baby almost seemed to cling of his own volition without any help from Sam, though some instinct he had previously not been aware of kicked in and his arms closed around the warm soft child, drooling against his T-shirt.

Sali stood in the tiny bathroom and scrubbed her arm with anti-bacterial soap and a nailbrush. Her heart was going way too fast and she felt completely out of kilter. She tried putting it down to her embarrassment at finding out the little hooligans, fruit of her womb, had robbed a neighbor, but she suspected it had more to do with the neighbor. At that shocking revelation she looked up into the mirror above the sink at her own wide-eyed reflection, seeing a smear of Albert's chocolate bar from his earlier kiss across her cheek, wild hair going every way, and eyebrows that desperately needed plucked. "Oh, crap," she whispered in agony to herself. Taking as long as she dared, she finally emerged, hair brushed, face wiped clean, and arms scrubbed. She took a deep breath and prepared to deliver the little speech she had practiced just as the front door banged open and 5 sets of feet barreled into the cottage, five voices crying out for "Mama" and five dirty faces stopped, staring in open-mouthed wonder at the man standing in their hallway holding baby Samuel.

Sali composed her face with a serious maternal scowl and introduced her offspring to Sam; "These are my children, Mr. Thompson." Pointing at the tallest child, a dark-haired boyish miniature of Sali herself, "This is Albert and he's 9, next is Stephanie," a slight girl with glasses and light brown hair glanced up nervously, "who is nearly 8.

Bridget is," Sali was momentarily nonplused, "Bridget is... hmm, how old are you Bridget?" The sturdy, outgoing child smiled, showing off two missing teeth and shouted, "I'm six and a half!" Sam winced at the shrill voice and marveled that such a noise could come from such a small creature.

"Where was I? Oh, yes, William here is five and Josephine is four." The smallest of the group huddled together looking guiltily up at their mother. "You are holding the baby, Samuel who is but nine months old." At that Sam was startled into remembering that he was, in fact, holding onto the small, warm child who had been held in fascination by the wire rimmed glasses just within reach balanced on Sam's straight, masculine nose.

"My namesake!" Sam remarked for lack of anything other to say in the face of such a tremendous group of hooligans. At that, the baby grabbed for Sam's glasses knocking them from his nose. Bridget took a flying leap in their direction screaming, "I'll get 'em!" as Sali gasped in horror. Sam watched in amazement as the glasses tumbled through the air in slow motion and were gracefully caught in mid-air by Bridget who held them up triumphantly.

Sali reached out her arms for the baby who mirrored the action and Sam gratefully gave up his burden. Bridget handed over the glasses and for a moment, peace was restored and a strange quiet settle over the gathering in Sali's' small hallway.

Mentally shaking herself, Sali forced herself to go on, "Children, this is Mr. Thompson. He has moved in next door and has discovered that someone has made off with some of his boxes. Would any of you know anything about that?" She looked piercingly at each of the children in turn but their faces stayed innocent. Glancing nervously at Sam, she shrugged as if to say, now what?

Typical helpless female, Sam thought to himself. Where is her husband and the father of this brood? "Mrs. Kelley, perhaps when your husband gets home he can get to the bottom of this..."

"He's dead mister!" from small, loud Bridget and the other children nodded their heads in agreement. Josephine grabbed hold of the hem of Sam's T-shirt and tugging for his attention she whispered in a very small voice, "Are you Samuel's Daddy?"

Horrified, Sali pulled Josephine away, "Jo! No, Mr. Thompson is not Samuel's Daddy! For heaven's sake, I don't know what possesses them sometimes," she cried giving Sam a look of complete and utter mortification. Looking at her round, delicate face, surrounded by that mop of unruly hair, cluttered about with children of uncertain parentage, Sam decided he would check with his attorney about the legalities of full disclosure by the Real Estate Agent. Surely a band of roving, felonious children and their immoral mother would qualify as something he should have been told about before finalizing the purchase of the small craftsman cottage next door.

Albert suddenly erupted, "Shhh!" he hissed at his siblings. "This is the deal," he said. "See, the kids got to go through the boxes the old neighbors left out for charity. They left them on the back porch. So, when there were more boxes there they thought that it would be okay to go through those, too."

"They?" Sali questioned darkly, looking at her oldest son.

"Okay, okay. We all did it but we weren't meaning to be bad and it was all boring stuff anyway. It's all out back behind the shed. It was just dumb old books and big black CD disks and papers." Albert looked disgusted as though it was Sam's fault that the take hadn't been better.

Sam felt his face get hard and cold as he looked at the thin boy. "Those are first edition books, son and collectible phonograph records and manuscripts by famous authors!" By the expression on Albert's face it was obvious that he had no clue what any of those things were.

The children may not have understood how valuable the contents of the boxes were but they certainly understood that their new neighbor was not happy. Wordlessly they led him through the house, out the back door, across the overgrown and vibrantly green back yard, around a dilapidated shed created from found objects to a stack of boxes that looked familiar. Sam dropped to his knees, anxiously scanning the contents for damage or breakage and found reason to be thankful that the children hadn't been more interested. They apparently simply made a cursory examination and then abandoned the haul.

Sali had followed the group to the backyard and much to her surprise found herself seeing the yard through the eyes of the neighbor. A large tree shaded the whole back lot, the grass was ankle deep, or deeper, flower beds overflowed in bright splashes of color and a freeform goldfish pond now held 3 Popsicle stick rafts and a sinking one-legged Barbie doll. The shed was a conglomerate of things she and the children had salvaged from the city dump; part of a wooden fence, patch worked plywood, corrugated metal, and the best find of all: a billboard advertising Santa's visit to a nearby mall.

Sam ran his fingers through his dark hair causing it to spring up in spikes across his head. It was long past his bedtime and his legs were beginning to ache but he couldn't work up an appetite for sleep. Stretching he walked to the window and peered out at the house next door. All of the lights seemed to be on, a TV was blaring and movement in the backyard indicated someone hanging laundry at, he glanced at his watch, eleven at night. He shook his head in disgust and confusion; finally having found some financial freedom with the ability to choose just about any sort of lifestyle he would want, he had to pick a cottage in a small California town next to a house of hooligans.

Sali quickly and efficiently hung the small garments on the line she had strung between the house and a tree. The dryer had quit the week before and she couldn't afford to get it fixed just yet. In fact, she thought to herself, breathing deeply of the damp night air, maybe she would never get it fixed. This wasn't so bad, mindlessly pinning clothes to a rope in the backyard at midnight.

Just then a low rumble of thunder and one cold raindrop sent her scurrying back into the house. She stood in the kitchen doorway and watched the basket of clean laundry get pelted with the furious rainstorm. Mentally shrugging in resignation, she walked through the house turning off lights and the television, scooping up sleeping Bridget who had collapsed while watching a kid video, and tucking her into her bunk bed.

As each light switch was flicked off Sali felt a little calmer until, finally, by the light of the flashes of lightning, she made herself a cup of decaf and sat in the doorway watching the rain.

Noticing a lamp on in the spare bedroom of the house next door, Sali wondered anew what sort of man Sam Thompson was. Today was the first day she had even seen him, though the kids had spied on him some and told her interesting facts such as how he ate off of paper plates and recycled his cans. Sali grinned in remembrance of the kids' "archeological expedition" through the trash cans of the neighborhood. It was in this way that they knew all the secrets of the shady street. The Thompson trash can next door held paper plates (100 for $1.99) and no cans whatsoever.

Finally, as the thunder storm moved off south of town, the decaf forgotten and cold, Sali stood and stretched her back muscles, taking one last long deep breath of the rain freshened air. Tomorrow was another day and she needed all the rest she could get just to get through it.

Just as the sun peeked over the trees across the street Albert woke as quickly as he had fallen asleep. Eyes popping open wide, he startled Sali as she rummaged through the dresser next to the bunk bed looking for a clean onesie for baby Samuel. "Oh, you're awake early, Al!" she said in surprise.

"Mama, I had weird dreams about that man next door." He looked so serious and earnest that for one moment Sali's heart dropped to her toes imagining horrible possibilities.

"Like what?" she asked trying to sound casual, forgetting to breathe.

"I dreamed he lived with us and was making us French toast from scratch and you were laughing." Sali's eyebrows rose a fraction imaging such a scenario and then in shock that her sensitive son should even imagine such a thing in his dreams.

"Hmmm," she said stalling for time. "Well, what does that mean to you? Do you think you were missing Daddy?"

"No!" Albert's face grew even more serious. "He's nothing like Dad!" Sali had to agree with him there. The kids' dad, Spencer had been short, stocky and tough. His wheat-colored hair had usually been too long and his face had usually been too happy; happy with wine, women and song, though the kids didn't know that. It had been two years since he'd died crossing the street, coming home from his favorite bar, a hit and run statistic. All they knew was that Daddy had been happy and fun and had died. Then only six months ago Sali's brother had been in a car accident killing both himself and his wife, sparing their sweet baby Samuel. It was a wonder the kids weren't nervous wrecks and completely neurotic.

"Well then, I have no idea why you would even imagine Mr. Thompson making breakfast," Sali declared emphatically to try and hide her confusion over the foggy remnants of a dream she herself had experienced. All that was left of that nighttime adventure was a feeling of comfort and relaxation that was all tied up with her new neighbor.

Albert shrugged and rolled over to face the wall, dismissing his mother. His confidences were getting fewer and further between so Sali was thankful for the few moments of connection they had just shared, though she couldn't help feeling that she could have done better. Pulling a clean onesie from the drawer she went back to the task of dressing her wiggly nephew, baby Samuel, who was now her sole responsibility.

Sam woke from a strange dream of being in that aromatic kitchen next door, flipping slabs of tender French toast on a griddle while hungry smiling children waited pleasantly at the scrubbed oak table nearby.

He shook his head and rose painfully, wondering what sort of sick fantasy that was. The Kelley children were probably never pleasant and he couldn't imagine a nightmare worse than having to cook for such a large brood.

Carefully stretching his screaming muscles and tendons, he did his morning exercises, cursing again the accident that had damaged his athletic legs and removed any chance of having children of his own. Children, who, he was sure, would be ever clean, happy and well mannered. As effectively as a surgeon's knife, the burning wreckage had rendered him sterile, an accidental vasectomy, and ruined his dreams of hiking mountain trails and biking across America with a family of his own.

Standing at the range in the kitchen, waiting for coffee to perk, Sam looked out at the back yard. Neatly mown with ordered beds of flowers and civilized vegetables he glanced over at the Kelley yard and made quick comparisons. Already, at this early hour, that wild child Bridget was squatting down in the tall grass poking at something with a stick. Her hair hadn't seen a brush yet and her face looked as though she had gone to bed unbathed. Sam shuddered, judging Sali as an unfit mother for her casual methods.

Bridget looked up from where she was examining the roly-poly bugs she had uncovered from beneath a smooth rock and saw Sam at his kitchen window. She grinned and waved her stick in the air, "Hi there Mr. Tom Son!" Sam waved back weakly and tried to force a smile upon his face. "I found me some bugs! They're gonna be my pets!" Bridget was so pleased at this idea she was oblivious to the look of horror settling across Sam's features.

"Don't you think a cat or a dog would make a nicer pet?" Sam asked the girl, stepping out onto the back porch so that he wouldn't have to raise his voice.

"Oh, pshaw, Mama won't let us have a cat or a dog. She says Baby Samuel is animal enough for us."

Sam recoiled. The woman was simply too much. Referring to her own baby as an animal and refusing the other children an ordinary pet because of her own misdeeds was absolutely the limit. He made up his mind then and there that he would have nothing further to do with her or her band of feral children. Bridget was now pressed against the simple picket fence that separated the properties holding out her hand, which was full of what appeared to be brown beads. Sam was intrigued in spite of himself and walked closer to the edge of his yard. As he watched, one of the "beads" unrolled itself and started crawling off across the grubby hand.

"See," Bridget pointed out, "they roll right up so we call 'em roly polies. But that one unrolled so's she can go home to her babies. Mama always says we have to let 'em go 'cause their babies would miss 'em if we kept 'em."

A startling revelation presented itself as Sam imagined his dark-haired neighbor instructing her children on the proper etiquette of bug collecting. That she would consider how the baby bugs might feel bereft of their mother amazed him and he tucked the thought away in the corner of his mind for later and deeper thought.

Sali was washing dishes; scrubbing congealed egg from breakfast, listening to Stephanie read slowly and painfully from a 2nd grade reader. As she washed, she moved her foot about to entertain Samuel who played at her feet, and kept one ear cocked to the sounds of Will and Jo in the bedroom.

Suddenly she noticed Bridget out back at the fence. Her Mama Radar zoomed in and she immediately grasped that her most outgoing child was talking with Sam Thompson. "Oh dear!" she exclaimed as she dropped the dish she had been scrubbing, swooped up the baby in her sudsy hands, and pushed past Stephanie to the back door.

"Bridget! Don't bother Mr. Thompson, dear!" Sam's head shot up and took in the scene, overlarge T-shirt, baggy shorts, baby wearing only a one-piece sort of body suit thing with bubbles clinging to its chunky thighs, and the child called Stephanie at her side holding a book. This unkempt woman was the same one who had advised that baby bugs would miss their mama and Sam found it hard to stay disgusted.

"It's all right. She's showing me her rolling bugs."

"Roly *poly* bugs," Bridget cried in glee at having opportunity to correct an adult.

"Begging your pardon, Madam!" Sam said in his best parody of a British accent, much to the delight of both Stephanie and Bridget. They laughed hysterically all out of proportion to his stab at childish humor. Something softened in Sali, watching this very uptight looking man joke with her daughters, and their obvious pleasure at being joked with. But on the heels of the softening came a sharp, bitter pain. Her daughters would never know the pleasures of having a father to flirt and joke with. How different life would have been had she listened to her parents and made a wiser marital match.

Sam watched the soft look of love cross Sali's features as she watched the girls laugh, but as suddenly as it came it left to be replaced with a tightening of her mouth and a look about her eyes as though she might cry. He was instantly contrite, not knowing what he had done to hurt her feelings, he impulsively continued the British accent charade, "and does your mum know what you're doin' dearies?"

"Aye," cackled Sali, getting into the spirit of the game in spite of her sorrow, "me thinks this bloke is bein' taken fer a ride by the wee sprites!" Her eyes met Sam's over the heads of the girls but instead of laughing an electrical current seemed to pass between them.

Bridget looked from one to the other and caught her sister's eye, winking in conspiracy. "Can I see your house Mr. Tom Son?" Bridget asked. In shock, Sam looked at her wondering where in the world that had come from. Sali hurriedly said, "Mr. Thompson is too busy, honey and besides you were in that house before when the Harrisons lived there."

"Pleeeeze," the child begged. Not knowing what to do,

Sam agreed and stood looking stupidly at her as she held her grubby arms up to be hoisted over the fence. When it dawned on him what was going on, he was nonplused by the whole situation, which had seemed to escalate out of his control. One moment he was merely watching a neighbor child play in her own back yard and now here he was lifting her over the fence to have tour of his new home.

Instead of dangling in his arms as he imagined she should have done, she seemed to cling to him like a baby monkey, all arms and legs wrapped around his torso in absolute trust. He leaned over to set her down on the grass in his yard but she was stuck tight and he found it necessary to peel her off of himself.

Meanwhile, her mother, the bug-sympathizing Sali, was hurrying with Stephanie around to the front gate before he could make off with Bridget into the dark reaches of his house. She smiled self-consciously at him but stood her ground and followed him and Bridget inside the back door.

The kitchen was devoid of any decoration, all appliance being black or white or chrome in stark contrast to Sali's own warmly wooden, family oriented kitchen. "Hey!" Bridget yelled causing Sam to jump and Sali to cringe in anticipation. "You don't have any pitures on your fridge! I can make you some so's it will be as pretty as my mama's!"

Sam's voice was calm and mcasurcd as he smiled at the tiny termagant and said that, of course, he would love some original Bridget artwork. Sali let her breath out, unconscious that she had even been holding it, in gratitude that he hadn't refused the offer and hurt the poor girl's feelings.

The tour continued through rooms as yet not unpacked or arranged, with the girls examining every last thing as though it were a treasure and never to be seen again. Sali found herself walking beside Sam through the living room, shoulders brushing and jerked in surprise. She argued with herself; the feeling had been altogether too pleasurable. She had no time for such entertainments and it was important that she keep her heart, head and soul focused on her children. There would be time enough when they were grown to feel those feelings again.

Shocked that she had felt such a jolt of pleasure over such innocent contact, she determined that it had been far too long since she had been around a man, except for Pastor Morris at church. It was proximity, that's all and the cure was to face it, ignore it and get over it. She smiled brightly and ignored the tingling in her body that seemed to magnetize her skin, attracting her closer to her sober faced neighbor.

Meanwhile, Sam had felt a jolt like the electrical storm of the night before run through his body when she brushed against him. How she managed to look so absolutely unkempt but smell so divinely of honeysuckle and spices was beyond him. "What's that fragrance you're wearing?" he asked impulsively.

Startled she looked at him in surprise; "I'm not wearing any unless you count the cinnamon and honey the kids got on me during breakfast. I made French toast."

Sam's dream came back to him, the vision of being in her kitchen surrounded by her children. He mentally shook his head to clear it and saw his house for what it was, a bachelor's residence. The family home he craved was beyond his reach because as much as he wanted it to be true, one man does not a family make, and he mourned again his sterility.

Chapter Two

Sali curled up in the big easy chair. She had reupholstered the stained piece of furniture after finding it at a second hand store in hideous condition. The smooth flowered chintz of muted, faded-looking shaggy roses against a gray-green background, was cool against her bare legs and she reveled in the sensation.

Albert, in a rare show of brotherly love, was reading to the little kids in the shade of the big tree out back. Earlier Sali had peeked out the kitchen window and had seen him sitting there, narrow shoulders leaning against the scratchy trunk of the elm while his brother and sisters listened intently to whatever story he was weaving.

Baby Samuel was curled up in his crib, fast asleep, and the house was cool, dark and quiet. With no pressing responsibilities making her feel guilty for just sitting she allowed her mind to wander.

In shock, Sali noticed the time. It was after nine and the dark wasn't shade, it was dusk. She marveled how time seemed to slip away so quickly. A day barely began before it seemed it was over and soon summer would be gone and the kids would be back at school. Well, at least most of them would be at school. Will would be starting kindergarten and Bridget finally in first grade full time. There would be only Jo and Samuel to keep her busy.

She supposed she ought to be thankful she had Social Security survivor's benefits and that the mortgage had had life insurance. All in all, with Spencer's death, she wasn't doing too badly financially. And she was ashamed to admit she barely missed him otherwise. He hadn't wanted to help with the children, being too busy partying to rock a baby or comfort a sick kid.

Though Sali believed that Spencer had loved the kids and even herself in as far as he was capable, that love didn't extend to displays of kindness or generosity. That side of his personality was protected in keeping for his friends when they went out to the bars.

Sali remembered one time in particular when Spencer was getting ready to meet up with friends for a night of partying. Stephanie had been a baby and Albert, not much older, was sick with the flu. He had it coming out both ends until eventually there were no diapers left and Sali had resorted to pinning hand towels to his bottom. At last, those were all dirtied too.

"Spencer," she had begged, "please go to the store and get some diapers before you go out." But he had refused. He had places to go and people to meet and his money was for buying drinks and hot wings, not for diapers. While Stephanie screamed, and Albert retched over a bowl with one of Sali's t-shirts pinned around his chapped little bottom, Spencer winked at Sali and was gone. That moment had been one of pure illumination and had changed her view of her husband forever.

Somehow they had weathered that night, and all the other unpleasant ones and now Sali could afford to be kind to Spencer's memory since he was gone. She could remember the good times for the kids and tell stories about him that put him in the best light and not feel the least bit resentful of their love for him. But, sometimes, when she was alone, or in the middle of the night when there weren't a million things to distract her, she would remember just how dreadful life with Spencer had been. And by contrast, how good life was now.

Leaning her head back against the flowered fabric, Sali felt her mind begin to drift. Riding on waves of pure sensation she felt the cool of a breeze and the satiny touch of skin on hers. It had been so long since anyone had loved her, she sometimes forgot she was a woman first and a mother second. A little moan escaped her lips as she rode the feeling of being touched and comforted, her mind strangely blank of all concern about children or food bills or broken dryers.

Sam had come at a gallop when he heard the first shriek. His heart had very nearly stopped, recognizing young Bridget's shrill little voice and locating it in space as coming from her backyard. He had catapulted himself from the back door, clearing the porch and the steps in one bound. He paused only for a fraction of a second once hitting the ground but another shriek followed the first and he braced his hands on the top rail of the picket fence and swung his body over into Sali's yard, the pain of his unused muscles and tendons screaming in agony.

The shadow of dusk was denser here under the heavy foliage of the tree but he made out the shapes of all of the older children huddled together trembling in fright. His own heart was racing by the time he breathlessly demanded to know if they were all right.

"Albert's telling us a good story!" Bridget exclaimed gleefully. Sam stared in disbelief while Albert quickly insisted it was only a little scary and he hadn't expected the kids to scream quite so enthusiastically.

"Where is your mother?" Sam asked with a chill to his voice, and the children, recognizing adult seriousness, silently pointed toward the house.

Sam found her curled up in a ridiculously flowered chair in the corner of the darkened living room. Her head was lying to one side, eyes peacefully closed and mouth trembling with a slight smile. Her loose shorts had ridden up her thighs, showing off an uninterrupted expanse of skin to the very edge of lace-edged panties.

Sam's mouth went dry at the sensations the sight of her provoked. Forcing a feeling of outrage at her being able to sleep through the children's terrorization at the hands of their older brother, he moved to shake her but found his hands caressing her upper arms instead. As though they had a will of their own, his hands moved gently over her soft skin, feeling the bands of muscle under his fingers.

Skin as soft as satin covering muscles as strong as steel was a combination that he had never considered sexy before but now that he had experienced it he decided it was extremely erotic. He felt as though he was being drawn closer to her until he was near enough to feel her breath on his lips and the smell of roses and baby powder that surrounded her. Her head moved slightly, her lips parted and a soft, sweet sigh escaped. Sam took his hands from her skin as though they had been burned. Bereft of the warmth of his skin her eyes flew open and saw his face inches from her own. "Oh!" she cried.

The children, standing behind Sam, waiting to see what would happen, stared in silent shock as their practical, calm, rational mother fluttered her hands nervously at her cheeks.

"I was, well, I was just..." Sam began. Simultaneously

Sali gasped.

Later that night, lying in bed after doing his physical therapy exercises, Sam pondered the experience. He had felt compelled to touch the woman, and he didn't know why. His hands seemed to itch with the need and he had had no control over the situation. His mouth had tingled with the desire to feel her soft lips under his. To breathe deeply of her scent was beyond his control. Thank goodness the kids had followed him in because, he told himself, he would have been hard pressed to back away had he not had an audience.

He shook his head as if to erase the memory of all those little faces looking at him like he was the bogeyman or something. When Albert had finally protested his innocence, claiming that he hadn't intended to scare the kids, it had snapped them all out of whatever spell they were under and they all spoke at once. Sam, saying he was checking to see if she knew that her children were screaming like wild banshees out in the yard, Sali saying she had only dozed off for a moment, baby Samuel calling out for someone, anyone, to come see to him. The situation was out of hand, Sam said to himself.

Again, he promised himself he would stay away from the house next door.

Sali, in her own bed, with Jo, Will and Bridgct surrounding her, mentally planned her grocery list, went over the month's budget and contemplated getting out the scissors and cutting the boys' hair. Anything to keep these errant thoughts from scrambling up her senses and mocking her responsibilities. How could she, a woman of 32 with five children and the task of raising her orphaned nephew become giddy like a school girl in the company of a middle aged man? It must be the isolation, she decided, once again trying to firmly put Sam Thompson out of her mind. But her errant mind kept straying to that moment before wakefulness fully arrived, when she could feel his hands on her arms. It hadn't felt like he was trying to shake her awake but more like he was caressing her with a tenderness she suddenly found she craved.

"Aarrgghhh," she groaned as she grabbed up a pad and began writing down a to do list for the next day.

The kids had been a little scared from Albert's story telling and used it as an excuse to sleep with her. As Bridget rolled over Sali rearranged the blankets. She had told as many happy stories as she could think of to get their minds on things other than ghosts and goblins and worms that grew fifty feet long and ate children, but in reality the kids had simply used their fear as an excuse.

The day would come soon enough when she wouldn't have the pleasure of being able to sleep with these warm little bodies and smell their clean skin for any reason. Enjoy it while you can, she said to herself with a grimace as she felt Will's fist hit her in the hip.

The list done, Sali smiled to herself, shifting away from the sweaty little bodies packed about her. Padding to the bathroom in the darkened house she filled the tub, using some of her secret cache of bubble bath and scented oils and lighting fragrant candles. Any day now Bridget would discover that the box of Epsom salts in the back of the linen cupboard really held exciting bath luxuries and then Sali would have to find a new place to hide them.

Being naked was a rare treat, she thought, grinning as she eased into the hot water. She leaned her head back and adjusted the hot water faucet with her left foot to keep a trickle flowing.

Continuing her memory of the time Albert was sick she recalled how Spencer had stumbled home in the middle of the night reeking of whisky, too loud with boisterous stories of tales told at the bar and jokes that could curl your hair. Sali had listened listlessly, rocking both children in her arms, and praying that his loud voice wouldn't wake them.

Spencer never became mean, and for that Sali could be thankful, but it had felt like he was just another one of the children. Irresponsible, foolish, a little stupid at times and needing her attention and care. In fact, she thought in sudden realization, sleeping with him had been just another thing done for him, like cooking his breakfast or telling the kids he had the flu when he was too hung over to smile much less laugh. Oh, she was sorry he had died - she wouldn't wish death on anyone - but she wasn't sorry the responsibility of him was no longer hers.

Moving her hand lazily in the water making ripples of sweet bubbles across her breasts she imagined what Sam Thompson would be like as a father. Though he looked terribly serious, he had joked with Bridget and been so patient with her. Bridget could be a trial, with her enthusiastic ramblings, but their neighbor had merely gone with flow of her thoughts and played along. And then his concern over the kids screaming in the back yard. That was touching, though he had not been impressed with her ability to sleep through the screams.

Mr. and Mrs. Harrison, the neighbors who had sold the house to Sam, had been as kind as grandparents since they had known the kids from their births on, and understood how tough it was for Sali all on her own. She supposed she was a little spoiled and now would have to curb the youthful exuberance emanating from her house in order to placate her new neighbor.

Her bath finished, Sali dried off and powdered her damp skin with perfumed talc. One last moment of nudity, stretching her back and sides, she slid her cotton nightgown over her head and trundled back to her room. In the muted moonlight coming through the lacy curtains she looked down on her three youngest children, curled like sleeping puppies this way and that across her double bed.

Carefully extricating a spread from beneath Bridget who was now sideways at the foot of the mattress, Sali padded into the living room and curled up in her flowered chair to sleep in peaceful solitude.

As the summer wore on, the days grew hotter. Sam managed to get his house into some semblance of order and took up a daily walk at dawn. He found that it helped his injured muscles more than just the stretching exercises alone and as his body grew stronger his walks grew longer until he knew the streets of the little town as thoroughly as if he had grown up there.

The old neighborhoods of tiny craftsman cottages had deep backyards and sidewalks that tipped and rolled like the deck of a ship. A few big elms still survived to hang shaggy, shady heads over the streets and yards and rooftops.

The Hill, a group of several streets on the highest spot of town, boasted larger homes that had been at one time, the height of luxury but now were just big old houses.

The newer avenues of cookie-cutter houses, 3 different models taking turns as they marched straight in perfectly engineered rows, were all stuccoed and painted beige or cream with brown trim. Sam found it fascinating to see how each family had tried to make their home unique. One with flowers, another with a banner proclaiming "Welcome" and many with bikes, trikes and toys strewn about the tiny front yards.

As a reward, every morning Sam stopped in at an old fashioned diner in the business district. It looked like something from a 1950's idea of a futuristic building, all curved walls and ribbons of blue and red fluorescent lights.

Amazingly enough, the coffee there was gourmet and professionally brewed. Sipping from a thick white mug he shamelessly eavesdropped on the voices around him. Tough workers having breakfast on their way to a factory, retired men on their own daily walks, and women meeting for a moment of sanity before their summer-frantic children demanded their time.

In an earlier life, before the accident that had changed his body and destroyed his dreams of future and family, he would have known those factory workers. As a part of management at a plant that manufactured industrial machinery components he had been required to understand every aspect of the process and was familiar with the names, faces and families of his employees.

It was ironic, he thought, that the very accident which had ruined his life had also rewarded him with enough money so that he would never have to work again, thanks to clever investing and a newfound gift at money management. But, as he was rapidly discovering, managing his money was a poor substitute for the dreams he had lost.

Growing up as an only child, Sam had craved the homey, family feeling that prevailed in his friends' houses. Their Christmas trees covered with homemade decorations intrigued him. Picnics and softball games in the local park were heaven to him but his own parents had careers that required attendance at higher social events. His attorney father and School Board Trustee mother were too busy to spend time on such frivolous pursuits.

After one last look around at the other patrons of the diner, Sam threw a couple dollars down on the counter and swiveled the turquoise-plastic covered stool away from the Formica counter. Other faces briefly glanced at him and then away; he was beginning to be a fixture here. Perhaps that was the first step to belonging.

Before the accident, Sam had lived in a condominium in the city, commuting each day to the factory in an industrial area. His neighbors were nameless faces he met in the parking garage or passed on the landscaped walk to the tennis court. He had dated occasionally; women with careers who wore silk dresses to fairs and makeup to the beach. Saturday nights were spent at art gallery shows and little jazz joints where he always felt just a little out of place.

Walking briskly back down his street toward home, Sam saw Bridget swinging on the gate next door. "Hi there, Bridget," he called to the wild-haired girl. He noticed that her usual sunny face was looking a little ragged around the edges. Squatting down to her level he could see that there were the salty tracks of dried tears on her plump, sun-bronzed cheeks. "Hey, what's wrong?" he asked instinctively lowering his voice to a level for serious confidences.

"I got in trouble," the child said mournfully, hanging her head in abject shame. "Mama left her bath pretties down and I was only gonna take a little bath with 'em but the whole bottle spilled and it made lots of bubbles and then..." She gasped for breath before going on. "...The bubbles went over on the floor and I rubbed the oil into my knees 'cause they're scabby from where I skinned 'em running after Jo when she took my roly poly and I slipped in the oil and spilled the powder." Peeking a look at Sam from under her amazingly long lashes he was surprised to see that, contrary to what he would have imagined, she was truly contrite and ashamed.

"And what did your mother do when she discovered the mess?" he asked, curious to find out how his neighbor treated her children.

"She cried."

Rocking back on his heels Sam felt like he'd been punched. The woman had cried. She hadn't screamed or hit or sent the child to a corner to suffer alone. She had cried. Probably those "bath pretties" were luxuries she seldom indulged in. He imagined her seeing her things wasted, the mess that would require her attention to clean up, oil and powder undoubtedly being difficult to remove quickly, the baby trying to get into the mess, all with the hooligans running about. Just as suddenly, unbidden came the image of her enjoying those luxuries, soaking in a bath of hot bubbles with her skin pink and shiny wet.

Shaking his head to clear the vision, Sam awkwardly patted Bridget plump shoulder. "What do you suppose you could do to make it up to your mother?" he asked.

The tearful face cleared like the sun coming out on a cloudy day, bright and shining with hope she whispered with barely contained excitement, "We could buy her more!" Sam noticed that Bridget has said "we" and not "I" and figured that this might be some childish manipulation.

"I don't think your mother would feel very comfortable with me taking you to the store, Bridget."

"Let's ask!" she shouted, racing up the walk toward the door, with Sam reluctantly following. It was amazing, he thought to himself as he traced the child's steps across the living room, into the hall and to the door of the bathroom, that for having vowed to stay away from the drama of this household he sure was familiar with the layout.

Bridget, quivering with excitement stood before Sali who was on her hands and knees in the tiny bathroom. Mopping up the clumped, oily powder with a sponge she looked every bit as upset as her daughter had implied. A squeal brought to his attention that the baby was ensconced in the empty and now clean and dry bathtub with a stuffed toy. Gleefully raising his dimpled arms, and smiling his nearly toothless smile, he appeared to recognize Sam and want to be held. Without any conscious thought he leaned down and swung the baby into his arms while listening to Bridget's patter.

"Mr. Tom Son wants me to go to the store with him. Can I? Huh? Can I? Pleeeze?"

Sali looked up at Sam suspiciously, wondering why he could possibly want to take Bridget anywhere, much less a store where she was sure to beg for gifts. "Why?" she addressed Sam, warily.

"Uh, well, um... I was going to buy some things and Bridget asked if she could go." He knew he looked guilty as hell but it didn't occur to him that Sali might think his guilt was of a more nefarious source than simply trying to keep a gift a secret, until she glared at him with absolute disgust.

"I don't think so," she stated with measured, clipped words, eyes narrowed in her delicate face.

Suddenly Sam felt a shove from behind nearly causing him to drop the baby onto Sali, and then crowding around his sides peeked Albert, Stephanie and Will looking curious and amazed to find their neighbor standing in the bathroom holding baby Samuel and watching their mother scrub the floor.

"Mr. Tom Son is gonna take me to the store to buy... it's a secret!" Bridget shouted to the other children. "Wanna come, too?"

Sali looked from her daughter's flushed and excited face to Sam's and reassessed the situation. Adults who had secrets with children were not to be trusted but it would be pretty hard for him to get up to no good with all the children along. She smiled as she imagined him trying to keep track of her brood.

Sam watched Sali's face go from anger and disgust to something akin to evil glee. *What was she thinking now?* he wondered, and felt a little thrill of apprehension shiver up his spine. Meanwhile, the other children began shouting that they too wanted to go to the store with Mr. Tom Son and buy a secret.

Sali hushed them and with laughter making her voice musical said, "You can all go. That is okay, isn't it, Mr. Thompson?" she asked primly.

Nodding numbly he found himself being led off with the four older children in tow, only little Jo and the baby left behind.

Sam decided to walk the children to the nearby shopping district and spare his car their sticky fingers. They set off back up the street with Bridget trotting here and there, looking in every yard, behind every bush and under every rock for "pets." Albert, walking beside him, tried on an adult look of indulgence at his younger sister. "She's pretty active," he commented and Sam assumed he was repeating something his mother had said before.

"Yes, I would agree with that." Sam smiled at the image they made, he tall and distinguished and they disheveled and slightly mucky with Bridget resembling a terrier on a leash let out for a daily run, darting from one spot to another.

The store that looked most promising was a Bed and Bath place that sported lacy curtains in the window with a display of pastel bottles arranged on delicate baskets and tiny steamer trunks. Sam stopped the group, holding the door shut with one hand while he looked at them sternly. "Now, you mustn't touch anything and we all will stay together." They nodded in unison, a little awed by the elegance of the store and quietly let themselves be led inside the dim store where pools of light illuminated displays about the interior.

After much discussion and sniffs of fragrance here and there the children began to get somewhat animated and Sam decided that the choice should be made soon before he lost their attention.

"What about this," he asked holding up a cut glass bottle of honeysuckle scented bubble bath. The kids nodded agreeably and at the suggestion of a helpful, tastefully dressed saleslady they gathered up some matching talc, oil, and candles. Noticing the miniature steamer trunks were lockable, on impulse he added one to the pile.

"What's that for?" Stephanie asked in her quiet, shy voice.

"That is so Bridget can't get to your mother's bath pretties ever again," Sam said firmly and Bridget had the good sense to remember that this shopping expedition was caused by her own recklessness.

The saleslady leaned forward as she put Sam's change into his hand and observed, "It's not often I see a group of children out with just their father. You're to be commended."

He felt his eyebrows raise fractionally in surprise and then was astounded to note that her assumption made him feel good. He looked down on the 4 brunette heads no higher than his elbow and realized that he was enjoying himself.

The walk home was slower. The kids told Sam stories of people who lived in the houses they passed, pointing out the spot where a injured dog had once been found. Rescued by Sali, the animal had been nursed back to health at the local veterinarian's office. Albert identified the places where the very best trick-or-treat goodies were handed out every year while Stephanie cataloged the costumes they each had worn for the last 3 years.

By the time they neared his house his legs were beginning to ache from the extra exercise but he found himself strangely reluctant to end the outing. "How about we go to my house and put all the goodies into the trunk so your mom will have to open it up with the key?" The kids enthusiastically agreed.

Never in his wildest dreams would Sam believe he would entertain such a motley crew of children in his spotless kitchen, but they made themselves at home, eagerly drank the lemonade he offered, and only made one mess when Will's glass tipped over.

They all helped to carefully set the bottles inside the box, and making a solemn procession they walked next door with Bridget in the lead carrying the trunk.

Sali was in the kitchen mixing up some egg salad for lunch sandwiches while Samuel banged a spoon on a pot lid and Jo helped by fetching things from the refrigerator. She looked up in surprise as the group approached. "What a pretty box! What's it for?" she asked Bridget.

Suddenly shy, Bridget nearly whispered, "It's for you. It's the secret."

Sali wiped her hands on a dishtowel and sat down at the old oak kitchen table while the trunk was set in front of her. She tentatively tried to open it and lookcd up in confusion when she found it was locked. Sam silently handed her the miniature skeleton key.

As the lid was lifted and Sali saw what was inside her eyes filled with tears and the children immediately began talking all at once. "It's for you, Mama!" Stephanie surprised herself by declaring loudly. Sam stepped back so that they could all reach their mother, hug her, and admire anew the contents of the trunk.

Sali raised her face from the eager kisses of her children and found her eyes looking into Sam's. They gazed unblinkingly at each other for several seconds until Bridget's demands for attention caused them to break contact.

Flustered at what had just happened, Sali thanked each child, and then turned back to Sam, careful to avert her eyes, "Thank you, Mr. Thompson, since I assume you paid for this generous gift."

"Hey, now," he said with a smile, trying for a lightness that was difficult to achieve, "isn't it about time you called me Sam?"

"Sam." Her voice seemed to caress his name and he had a brief moment to wonder why his heart was beating so fast or why his mouth was suddenly dry.

"Would you like to stay for lunch, Sam?" she asked, and he nodded to avoid speaking in fear his voice would come out raw and hoarse with some undefined need.

After every calm spot, a rough one usually follows, and vice versa, Sali told herself. The rest of the day had been a blur of cranky kids wanting any excuse to visit their neighbor. Sali's nerves were frazzled and when the last child was tucked into bed she ritualistically carried the little steamer trunk to the bathroom. The water was perfect, the bubbles thick and rich, the scent reminiscent of summer nights and the candles made a pleasant flicker on the walls.

Leaning back in the water she luxuriated in the sensation of having been treated kindly, finding it a much greater present than the material gifts.

Next door, in the glow of lamplight, Sam listened to some mellow, modern, instrumental music on the stereo but found his mind gravitating to the house next door. He could see the flicker of candlelight coming from the bathroom window and he imagined Sali lying back in the tub. A tightening in his groin startled him and he groaned in disgust. He was lusting after his motherly, bohemian neighbor, for heaven's sake!

She was as different from the type of woman he used to date as anyone could be. He had always seemed to end up with calm, self-possessed women, their bodies model thin and sleek. Voices well modulated, they talked of who they knew and what they had. In fact, he realized with surprise, those women had been very much like his mother.

Irritated with himself he rose and quickly changed CD's for another that was handy. The Beatles singing "Lady Madonna, children at your feet, wonder how you manage to make ends meet..." sent him to the window where he stared over at Sali's house and hoped that she was having a nice evening and that the kids hadn't been too wild, and wondered how she managed to make ends meet.

Chapter Three

The car wouldn't start. It simply wouldn't start. Sali turned the key again and heard the ominous grinding noise that even she, in her infinite automotive ignorance could recognize was about a $200 repair. All six kids were clean, dressed neatly and with hair not only brushed, but in the case of the girls it was done up in braids and ribbons. They were sitting belted in the vehicle around her and set to go if only the old green car would cooperate. For one moment Sali bowed her head and rested it against the steering wheel in abject misery. I just can't believe it, she thought to herself. *It's punishment for being so satisfied lately; I just know it.*

"Are you praying, Mama?" Bridget questioned in her shrill voice. "Can't you wait till we get to church?"

"The car won't start, Bridget. If the car won't start we'll have to walk to church or skip it like we did last week." Sali knew that the children looked forward to Sunday School every week, and she hated to disappoint them but walking them all there while keeping them clean was a task she didn't often succeed at.

Trying once more, the grinding noise seemed slower, as though the battery was wearing down and she cast a self-conscious eye toward Sam's house just in time to see him twitch the curtains shut.

Gathering her purse, the diaper bag, the snack bag, the toy bag and all the other paraphernalia the children saddled her with, she was startled when the car door suddenly opened next to her.

"Oh!" she exclaimed looking up at Sam as he leaned down with his face inches away from hers. She noticed his eyes were brown with topaz streaks behind the wire-rimmed glasses and he must have just shaved because there on his right cheek was a remnant of shaving cream.

"Having trouble?" he asked raising his eyebrows at the pile of canvas and straw bags she still held clutched in her fist.

"My guess is that it's the starter. C'mon kids, let's go. If we're going to walk we'd better get a move on." Sali noticed that he stepped aside but not very far so that she had to swing her legs out and put one foot on each side of his nearer denim clad thigh. With one hand braced on the top of her door and the other on the top of the car, his shirt was pulled tight across his upper arms. Even through the material she could see that his thinness was deceiving; there were bands of sinewy muscles there and she wondered what the rest of him looked like without clothes covering him.

"I'll take you," Sam surprised himself by saying quietly.

While Bridget and Will sang "hallelujah" and Albert scrambled to unfasten baby Samuel from his car seat, Sali realized that she was still staring at Sam's chest. Dragging her eyes away with effort she mumbled, "That's really not necessary."

"I suppose I should ask where you're going but with all these adorable children," he paused for effect, wagging his eyebrows at Bridget who grinned back, and got a fresh chorus of "hallelujah's" from the back seat, "I would have to hazard a guess that you're heading to church. Albert, give me the baby and you can detach that seat so we can put it in my car." Noticing Sali's expression, one of shock with a little outrage thrown in, he added, "And I know it isn't necessary but I'd like to give you a ride."

He moved back to give her more room and noted that she was wearing a simple dress that flattered her figure and showed off her legs. Because of the heat she wasn't wearing hose but her strappy sandals and swinging earrings dressed up the outfit enough for church. Where the sun created highlights in her hair, it glowed with a hint of auburn, and it's usual wildness was tamed into a clip at her neck.

Parked in the driveway at the side of the house, Sam's car was a four-door sedan, large and comfortable with soft upholstery. Crowding around an open door, they all admired the interior but the truth was there were simply not enough seat belts and Sali's rule was that everyone must be belted in before the car moved. Groans of disappointment all around made Sam almost sorry he'd even offered the ride. It had never occurred to him that there would come a time when his full-size car wasn't large enough.

"We'll walk," Sali said in a weary voice. She sent Albert to the shed out back for Samuel's stroller while herding the kids out of Sam's driveway and toward the sidewalk.

Stephanie tugged on Sali's dress causing her to lean down nearer the child's mouth, "If you want to bring the cart I'll pull Will and Jo so we can go faster," she whispered.

"Good idea, Stephanie!" Rewarding the child with a smile, Sali added, "Why don't you run get it?" The old, rusty red wagon would do in a pinch.

"Mine is larger." Sam's mouth quirked in a small smile

and Sali wondered if he was being flirtatious, in front of all the kids, no less.

"Your what is larger than what?" Sali asked sharply almost afraid to hear his answer and feeling a blush betray where her errant thoughts were taking her.

"My cart. I have a large wagon I planned on using for hauling garden supplies around but it hasn't been used yet and is quite clean. We can put three kids and all the bags in it, I'm sure. But it'll be pretty heavy for a child to pull so I'll pull it." He seemed pleased with his idea and Sali hadn't the heart to shoot him down in defense of her own sense of responsibility.

Soon Jo, Will and Bridget were sitting in style within the high slatted sides of the four-wheeled garden wagon. Samuel was gleefully belted into his stroller and Albert and Stephanie solemnly matched the pace that Sali and Sam, in spite of a slight compensation for his injured legs, set for the group.

"What do you have in all those bags?" Sam asked once they were underway.

Sali looked at the canvas, cloth and straw bags she carried with her pretty much everywhere and laughed. "Well, the string bag has toys in it. That's to keep the kids occupied if they get bored or wiggley. The canvas bag is full of diapers and a change of clothes for the messier kids." Sali paused to tuck Jo's hand back into the cart away from the wheels. "The straw bag is for snacks. I keep some bottled water, a baby bottle, some dried fruit, crackers, baby wipes for sticky fingers, and uh..."

"That's enough! I had no idea that taking kids anywhere would require so much *stuff!*"

"Well, it doesn't usually but going to church is challenging. They get bored and it's near to lunch time and they really can't talk or wiggle."

The kids began singing a song about ants marching one by one making any further conversation impossible. Was he going to come in with them? Sali asked herself. Frantically, she started going over in her mind some seemingly unrehearsed replies she could make when the busybodies at church commented on Sam's presence, but everything sounded idiotic. She was so busy thinking she didn't even notice that they were rapidly approaching the tree-shaded front doors of the old chapel. Because of their late start, services had already started so they unloaded the kids and lined them up in preparation for entering the quiet sanctuary.

Sam had a moment's unease when he realized that he had no good excuse for not attending church with the Kelleys. He would be entering the chapel wearing jeans and a simple cotton shirt. Thankfully he had shaved this morning, not always a given on Sundays, but he felt underdressed and out of his element. He glanced at Sali and saw that she looked just as uneasy. *Did his attire embarrass her?* he wondered.

He was so out of his element here. Now, if it had been a cocktail party he would have known what to do and how to act. But church? In a small town? With a bunch of kids? Taking a deep breath, he decided that if he faked it with the appearance of self-confidence, he could pull it off.

The outer doors stood open to the foyer and the interior double doors opened with only a slight creak. It took a second for Sali's eyes to adjust to the dim lighting, and they all paused while she peered about for an empty row. The entire congregation had heads bowed in prayer and just as Sali silently pointed to an empty pew near the back on the left, the Pastor gave a heartfelt "Amen" and all heads raised as one, turning to look at Sali's group.

Sam smiled confidently, nodding to the sea of strangers' faces, as his stomach clenched with nerves. Suddenly a return of the surge of pride he'd felt the day before in the store when the saleslady had mistaken him for the children's father washed over him. Every child was clean and neat, though Bridget's bow was now cock-eyed and Will's neat white shirt had come untucked.

Sali, however, did not share his pride. She felt the blood drain out of her face and then rush back to heat her cheeks, when she saw that her family was the object of the attention of every parishioner.

The sermon was blessedly short and lively with lots of songs and hops up and down until the call for children to go to Sunday School while the adults stayed behind for a more in-depth lecture.

As soon as the kids filed out Sam scooted down on the pew until he was right next to Sali and the baby. She had the bag of toys, cloth books and dolls, open and Samuel was digging through it in slobbering glee. One terry cloth clown flew from his grasp landing on the floor and Sam reached down to retrieve it. Inadvertently his forearm brushed Sali's calf and she gasped in pleasurable shock.

He quickly looked up at her face and found himself unable to draw away. Even as he sat back up and handed the clown to Samuel he stared at her until she felt her cheeks growing hotter. Finally breaking his gaze, she bounced the baby as though he was upset even though he had been perfectly satisfied and not at all fussy.

The children were ushered back in to meet up with parents, and Sam moved down the pew to make room for the Kelley kids to sit between him and Sali. One last prayer and it was over. Sali tried to make a fast getaway; she hurried the kids, whispering frantically for them to move along. Albert glanced at her in confusion, knowing that she always looked forward to the visiting out front on the grass after Sunday services and usually took her time greeting friends and acquaintances.

Today she seemed to want to leave without even shaking the pastor's hand and her lips got tight and mad looking when Sam clasped the plump cleric's hand.

"Well, well, I don't believe we've met!" Pastor Morris said in a booming voice, more used to projecting from the pulpit than engaging in normal conversation.

Introducing himself, Sam carefully avoided any explanation of his relationship to Sali and the pastor's eyes darted from one to the other in speculation before moving on to the next person in line, eager to shake hands and exchange a few pleasantries.

Sali had already reached the wagon and stroller before Bertha Browning, an older woman and the neighborhood busybody, managed to halt her progress and try to ferret out the situation. "Hello, Sali, dear. How are you and your sweet children?"

"We're just fine, Mrs. Browning, thanks. And how are you today?" Sali said with the slightest sigh of irritation. Seeing Sam rapidly approaching she started strapping the baby into the stroller, and looking about distractedly for the other kids.

"I see you have a friend visiting with you today..." Mrs. Browning raised her eyebrows and licked her lips in anticipation of juicy gossip.

Just at that moment Sam reached Sali's side and immediately saw that she was nervous. Perhaps with her reputation for being of questionable morals in the past, Bridget wasn't even sure who the baby's father was, for goodness sake, Sali was afraid that the other church members would think she had backslid back into her loose ways. Feeling protective of her, he smiled his most charming smile and introduced himself yet again. "I've moved in next door to

Sali's family and been adopted by her children," he explained.

Mrs. Browning's eyebrows rose even further, if possible, and looked unbelievingly at Sam before Sali abruptly made excuses and called to the other children. Sam helped Bridget, Will and Jo into the wagon and they made their way back to the house slowly, Albert and Stephanie dawdling as though to draw the time out.

As they neared the house Sali instructed the children to get out of their Sunday clothes and put on play clothes. Sam was hoping he would be invited for lunch again, but instead she made a curt good-bye with no excuses and disappeared inside, leaving Sam standing on the sidewalk with his garden wagon and the feeling that he had disappointed her in some way. Shaking his head slowly, he pulled the wagon up his driveway and contemplated how lonely the rest of the day seemed to stretch before him.

Watching through the bedroom window as Sam put the wagon away in his garage at the end of the driveway, Sali wasn't sure why she had been so uncomfortable about her neighbors seeing her with him. She felt like so much of a mother that it was almost indecent that they might consider for even one moment that she could be a woman with passions or that a man might find her attractive.

Not that one did, she assured herself. Sam Thompson was a nice man and he apparently liked her children; she was just along for the ride, an unfortunate bit of baggage to be endured so that he could enjoy Bridget's prattle and Albert's serious observations. And why that made her feel so sad and lonely she couldn't really say.

Sali had decided after Spencer died that she was going to stay single until her kids were all grown. Romance was for the birds; she had more important things to do, like raise these kids and after they were all in school she wanted to find out what she liked and who she was

As a kid she had liked to garden and her family had considered her quite talented. Squatting down in a freshly tilled planting bed, she had found the smell of damp earth exciting. Listening to the thirsty ground soak up life-giving water had brought her peace and contentment.

Vaguely Sali remembered her fantasies of making beautiful parks, living pockets of serenity and idyllic gardens. Perhaps that gift wasn't lost forever and she looked forward to the time when she could again have time to garden.

With a wry grin she considered her own yard now. Her parents would never believe it, that the green thumb she had sported as a child couldn't do more than produce straggly marigolds and weedy grass.

It was hard to do anything other than be a mom with a crew like hers. Sali's parents couldn't really understand it. They had had just the two kids and though Sali's mother had been a stay at home mom until the kids were in school, she had had her own interests and activities.

After retirement, they had moved to Florida where Sali's father took up sailing and Sali's mother belonged to several clubs and regularly had lunch with friends. She was always urging Sali to get out more, meet a man, and fall in love.

Romance just took your mind off of your responsibilities or else your responsibilities took your mind off of romance, Sali wasn't sure which. But they didn't mix, that was for sure.

Spencer had thought her a stick in the mud as the kids started coming. The things they had done together as a couple before Albert was born seemed tawdry and juvenile to her once she was a mother.

Sali had never liked drinking or the atmosphere in bars

but she went along because she loved Spencer and wanted to be with him. After becoming a mother she loved her baby and wanted to be with him, and he needed her more and was so much more fun. Naturally, Spencer had complained that she, Sali, had changed, and he had been right.

So, why did the image of sleeping alone and of her being "only" a mother for the next 17 years and 2 months depress her today?

Sam had stopped to examine a flowering shrub next to his back porch, Sali noticed from her bedroom window. His shirt stretched tight over his shoulders and his backside was as tight and muscular as his thighs. It dawned on her that he had a slight limp to his walk and she wondered what must have happened to him. Maybe the kids would ask, and tell her. But why she should care she still hadn't figured out.

In a burst of energy, Sali decided to clean out the pond in the back yard. Pulling on a pair of shorts that were, even in her unconventional wardrobe, worn out and baggier than usual she chose a sleeveless tank top that would allow the summer breeze to cool her off during the task.

Using empty plastic margarine tubs the kids helped Sali bail out the old, brackish water from the pond. When Will accidentally splashed some of the greenish liquid onto Stephanie's foot the job became a water fight free-for-all. Before Sali knew what had happened she was drenched. It had been Bridget's errant splash that had done the deed and a dreadful silence fell over the group when they saw their mother gasp in shock as the water hit her. Arms held out to her sides, mouth frozen open in disgust, Sali looked at the kids' horrified faces. Suddenly she began to laugh.

Sam heard the laughter and stepped out on his back porch for a closer view. Sali was laughing with abandon.

Drenched, her threadbare tank top had molded itself to her body. Unable to stop himself he began laughing, too and the Kellys looked over at him. Momentarily embarrassed, Sali plucked at the bottom of her shirt, trying to pull it away from her breasts and feeling her nipples harden as the air hit them. When Sam continued to laugh she grabbed up her larger bucket full of pond water and with a wide swing tossed the fluid in his direction.

Sam's mouth was open, his head thrown back in mid-laugh when the water hit him, filling his mouth. Sputtering, spitting and coughing in horror he picked a piece of moldy grass off of his cheek and flicked a Barbie shoe from his shoulder.

Watching the stiffening of his shoulders, Sali involuntarily stepped back in alarm. Forgetting modesty she let go off her shirt and held her hands up beseechingly. "Now, Sam... it was just in fun."

He slowly stalked toward the fence and carefully put his long legs over the pickets one by one. Sali screeched one short burst and turned to run but he leapt upon her knocking her to the soft grass. As her air whooshed out he straddled her thighs, one hand on her back to hold her still. "Give me water!" he called to the kids. They were staring in fascination but Bridget quickly broke the frozen tableau by grabbing a tub of water and handing it to him. Slowly, with great relish, he dribbled it onto Sali's hair, and back, seeing that not only was it filthy, it had little bugs swimming about.

"Get the hose!" Sali yelled, squirming to get away. Bucking her hips she felt Sam's thighs tighten around her.

Somewhere in the back of his brain he knew he should get up but the sensation of Sali's rounded backside squirming beneath his thighs cause an instantaneous reaction. To get up now could be disastrous, shocking not only Sali but her children as well.

Albert's eyes narrowed. "Get off my mom," he growled. "She wants you to stop."

Sali stilled and looked over her shoulder at her oldest son. Sam raised up and reached down a hand to help her up. "Did I hurt you?" he asked. Carefully keeping his body bent over he plopped down on the grass until the physical evidence of their horseplay abated.

"No! No. Albert, we were just playing. He didn't hurt me. See, I'm okay." Sali again pulled the soaked shirt away from her body and brushed the wet tendrils from her face. "But I'm filthy! How about a clean water fight?"

Once the majority of crud was washed away with the hose Sali set a sprinkler up for the kids to jump through while she resumed cleaning the pond. The clean cold water did wonders for Sam's condition and after the impromptu shower he settled himself on the back steps in the sun, ostensibly to dry. Unobtrusively watching Sali as she dished out the rest of the water, shoveled out the muck and scrubbed the mossy sides of the small rock pond he laughed at the kids leaping antics in the sprinkler. When the pond was clean Sali refilled it and sat down next to Sam.

"Good job," he observed. "Will you put in fish or plants or anything?"

"I'd like to but I'm afraid they wouldn't survive long with this crew. For now it will just be water." She tilted her face to the sun and enjoyed the warmth on her work-dampened cheeks.

"How about a fountain?" he asked, imagining a little rock waterfall in the center.

"Maybe once I get the car fixed and the dryer fixed and the school clothes bought. That is if nothing else breaks down." Laughing at her tragic litany of woes, Sali stood stretched her back.

Sam wondered anew how she managed to make ends meet.

"Right now I think it's time for me to start dinner. I only gave the kids peanut butter and jelly sandwiches for lunch because I wanted to get started on the pond. They're probably starving." She hesitated, and then gathered her courage about her. "Would you like to stay for dinner?"

Sam looked at Sali's face, eyes turned away from his, cheeks slightly flushed, and realized that she was nervous. "I'd love to but only on one condition."

Sali's glance quickly met his. "What's that?"

"That you let me help."

Peeling potatoes, tossing a salad and shucking corn on the cob weren't challenging tasks for Sam but preferable to standing by the hot stove where Sali was frying chicken. The scent was reminiscent of his friend's homes when he was a kid. Sam's own mother would never have served anything as middle-class as fried chicken.

Sam remembered that as a child he had once invited a friend for dinner. His mother had planned a candle lit gourmet feast that might as well have been the muck Sali had just scraped from the pond out back for all that Sam enjoyed it. His friend had looked horrified at the vichyssoise, stuffed tomatoes, and extremely rare filet mignon. The poor kid had suddenly discovered that he had a Cub Scout meeting that night and left without taking a bite.

Sam had never invited another friend to his house. The cold, barren life of the only child of professional people had left its mark on him.

While Sali and Sam went about preparing dinner the kids settled down in the living room in dry clothes to watch a video. Albert, appeased now that he had been reassured that Sam hadn't hurt his mother, fiddled with some pieces from a clock that he had dismantled and strewn across the table.

Sam stopped his tearing of the lettuce for a moment. He was besieged by such a feeling of well-being and contentment that he deliberately catalogued it, so that he would remember the moment. He took in the sizzle of chicken cooking in hot oil, the low murmur from the VCR in the living room, the occasional giggle or childish comment and the motorized hum of a lawn mower somewhere in the neighborhood. He breathed deeply of the aroma of fried chicken and boiling potatoes, cut grass, and Sali. He knew a longing to belong to this family so great it frightened him and made him momentarily confused.

How could a frazzled woman with too many children, living in a crowded house, and beset with broken mechanics be attractive? He shook his head to clear it and went back to tearing lettuce into a huge crockery bowl.

Sam was standing behind her on her left and it made her nervous. Sali couldn't really pinpoint why it made her nervous but she could feel a shaky feeling in her belly and thighs that made her focus an inordinate amount of attention on the frying chicken. Usually she managed to do everything at once without a problem but at this moment it was all she could do to not fuss with the chicken so much she spoiled it.

Never, in her life, had she known a man to help in the kitchen. Not really help. Spencer certainly never had, and neither had her father for that matter. He would sit in his chair in the den, watching the news on TV, smoking his pipe, while her mother made supper. Later, when Sali was older, she helped her mother while her brother sat in the den with their father.

This, then was something outside of her experience. Of course, if she'd thought about it, she would have said that she wanted to raise her sons to be able to cook and clean but they had no role model. And weren't likely to acquire one, either, she reminded herself.

Risking a glance at Sam as he carefully diced celery, Sali wondered if just being a neighbor counted as a good role model. Could her boys benefit from Sam's proximity?

Sam saw movement from the corner of his eye and looked up at Sali. She held a set of cooking tongs in her hand over the sizzling frying pan, her hair had dried where she'd pushed it back from her face and now was as disarrayed as any sexy model's. Though her clothes were dry he held the image of her, soaking wet, shirt plastered to her ample breasts, rounded fanny bucking beneath his thighs.

"Ouch!" The knife had missed the stalk of celery completely and had taken off a slice of Sam's finger.

"Oh, dear!" Sali cried as she quickly grabbed his finger and shoved it under a stream of water at the sink.

"It's nothing. Just a nick." But the commotion had brought the children at a run. Bridget gleefully and liberally drenched the wound in peroxide and Stephanie applied a cartoon Band-Aid. Sali barely kept from laughing at the look of confusion on Sam's face while he submitted to their ministrations and wordlessly went back to the counter where she finished chopping the celery.

Chapter One

The diner was filled with people and the air was full of the sound of clattering dishes, orders to the cook and the low hum of constant conversation. Sam took up a place at the Formica counter and turned the waiting coffee cup right side up to signal the waitress, a dyed-blonde in a pink uniform, that he would have some java. She zipped by and filled the cup on the run, calling out to a large, middle-aged man on the other side of the room. "Just a minute, Jim. The hash browns are coming!"

Sipping the hot brew black, Sam stretched his long legs out as far as the limited space in front of his stool would allow and let his mind wander, picking up bits and pieces of conversation around him. In his solitary life he found the anonymous company of the diner comforting.

"Stella says I should frost a little on top," a woman's husky voice twanged from somewhere behind him.

From an unseen diner off to the left, "And then I says, if you can't give me that overtime, well, then, I quit," followed by a smoky masculine cough and an appreciative whistle.

"Yep. That's what I said, too. Heck, Spencer called her Saint Sali but I hear she's getting boinked by her neighbor," the man next to Sam said in a low voice. Sam's body went still with the effort of listening and it was all he could do to keep from leaning in the speaker's direction.

"Ah, c'mon. No way!" another man croaked. Sam risked a quick look, seeing that the men were two of the factory workers he had noticed from other mornings.

"I swear it's true! My mother-in-law goes to Sali's church and says she brung the guy with her last week. And he was pleased as punch to be there even with all those wild kids."

"So what makes you think he's getting any? Dang, man, the woman's a shrew. She spit out those babies year after year while old Spence worked his fingers to the bone on the assembly line just keeping 'em in diapers and baby food."

"Yeah. Till she killed him."

Sam's heart stopped. She killed him? He waited for more but the men had gone on to another topic, that of a recent softball game, and then they left to go to work. I knew it, he said to himself. No one normal has that many kids! On the heels of that thought was the realization that there were rumors that he was sleeping with Sali. For a moment he didn't even stop to wonder why that would give him such a proud feeling of manliness, he just basked in the pleasure of their assumption.

Before his accident he had dated, and certainly enjoyed his share of women's favors. Since that fateful day he had spent time recovering, then more time in physical therapy and now living in a new town where he didn't know any-one, he hadn't had any opportunity to ask a woman out. Sighing, he thought, *who am I kidding. I'm scared.*

In his mind, dating was enjoyable but it was a prelude to finding out if you would be compatible for life. And since most women wanted children, he couldn't imagine start-ing a relationship that he knew would die once it was found out that he couldn't produce the goods.

Ruefully, Sam considered that it was a sad day in his life when two factory workers could make him feel good about himself simply because they thought he was getting laid.

Walking home from the diner he tried to imagine how Sali might have killed poor old Spencer. Maybe it was excessive procreation, he joked to himself and actually laughed out loud causing a little old lady picking up her newspaper off the sidewalk to jump in fright.

Bridget spotted Sam before he noticed her and came running, short brown legs pumping as though her life depended upon it. "Sam, Sam!"

"What's wrong?" Sam's heart did a double flip flop as his mind conjured up myriad things that could go haywire at his erstwhile neighbor's house.

"Baby Samuel took seven steps all by himself!" She jumped about gleefully in unrestrained excitement and Sam found himself sharing her laughter, though he told himself it was relief that there were no new catastrophes.

"Isn't he a little young to be walking?" Sam asked Bridget, not knowing too much about such things but trying and failing to imagine Samuel's short, plump baby legs able to support that round, wobbly body.

Bridget adopted a look of superior knowledge. "Oh, my yes! Mama says he's a real genius."

The two conversed companionably about when each of the other kids had started walking, though Sam doubted her claim that she had walked at and talked at 1 day old. Bridget explained that she had to go inside and described what delectable thing Sali was making the kids for breakfast. Having never heard of Holy Eggs he was almost tempted to take Bridget up on her invitation to join the family but then remembered the look on Sali's face when he had last seen her on Sunday. She probably wouldn't appreciate a drop-in guest for breakfast, especially if Holy Eggs turned out to have some sort of religious significance.

"Why do you walk funny?" Bridget asked suddenly.

Sam's step faltered as he heard her question. "You mean my limp? he asked to clarify her question. At her nod he hesitated, considering if his answer would frighten her. "I used to work at a factory…"

"Oh, like my dad did?"

Sam nodded and continued. "There was a big machine that was broken and one day it blew up and I got hurt. It damaged my legs."

"Did you bleed?" she asked with ghoulish interest.

"Not much. Most of the damage was internal."

"What's 'internal'" Her funny little face screwed up as she tried to understand.

"That means 'on the inside.' I spent a long time in the hospital while the doctors tried to make me all better."

"Are you all better now?"

"They did their best but I still walk funny and I can't ever be a father." He stopped, realizing he was treading on thin ice.

"Because you got hurt?"

"Uh huh," Sam answered vaguely.

Patting the child's unkempt hair Sam said goodbye and entered his own gate as Bridget went on to the next yard, singing a song to herself about babies walking on tippy toes.

Quickly, using a small juice glass like a cookie cutter, Sali cut a hole in the center of a slice of bread. Dropping the slice onto the pan of sizzling butter, she efficiently cracked an egg into the hole. Albert insisted his yolk be popped and cooked hard. Stephanie didn't care and never complained so she usually got fed last after the other kids had complained about Sali's cooking skills. Bridget liked her yolk runny and Will preferred his with the yolk spread all over the bread. Jo loved extra butter to the point of nauseating greasiness and Samuel got scrambled no matter what. But the gist of it all was this: Sali was able, with one pan and minimal fuss, to prepare eggs and toast in a myriad of ways for her brood and they thought it was special. The last Holey Egg was served up on a plate just as Bridget came banging through the front door.

"Don't slam, honey!" Sali continued pouring milk and juice, exchanging a dinner fork for a salad fork for Will who had a propensity to accidentally stab his eyes, and then cutting Jo's Holey Egg into bite sized, gooey pieces.

"Guess what!" Bridget called out excitedly to the family but having played her games in the past they all ignored her, the silence stretching on.

Finally Stephanie, in a show of pity asked "What?"

Leaning forward conspiratorially Bridget squinted her eyes and whispered, "I know what happened to Mr. Tom Son to make him walk funny."

Sali's head shot up. Turning on her heel she looked intently at Bridget hoping the child would tell everything she had discovered without having to grill her. Grilling her would give the kids cause to wonder why Sali cared and from there, speculation in their childish ways of intrigue and high drama.

"A machine blowed up and hurt him really bad and he spent a long time in the hospital and now he can't have no kids of his own at all. So, I told him I would be his pretend girl and make him pitures for his fridge and let him see my report card and everything." She immediately began eating with gusto.

"That's stupid!" Albert muttered in disdain. "How can a machine blowing up make him not have any kids? He doesn't even have a wife."

"How do you know if he has a wife?" Stephanie asked.

Albert shook his head in a superior way. "Have you seen one?"

"I want to make pitures, too!" Will interjected loudly.

Sali looked at the kids arguing while her mind went down paths she'd rather not go down. He had been hurt in an explosion. He couldn't have children. My God, she shuddered, had his whole damn business been blown off?

"You can all make him pictures." Sali looked with new appreciation at her wild bunch. Little Samuel banging his rubber tipped spoon on the high chair tray, flipping bits of scrambled egg about. Jo and Will listening intently to the older kids. Stephanie and Bridget earnestly discussing the types of pictures that would be most appropriate for a man who would never have children of his own. And Albert, surveying them all in an adult way. She loved each and every one of them, even when they were horrid. They gave her a purpose and pleasure in life that she knew was not available in any other way. Trying to imagine a life with no kids, no hope of any kids was at once extremely intriguing and horrifying in its bleakness. Shaking her head she began wiping up Samuel's mess from the floor.

The next morning Sam came striding down the street from his walk, finding his mind dwelling again on the question of how Sali could have killed her husband. Meanwhile, Sali was in the front yard watering an overgrown flowerbed that consisted mainly of leggy carnations and seedy marigolds. "Hi there, neighbor!" Sam called in a hearty voice.

Steeling her features to what she hoped would pass for nonchalance, Sali turned and smiled. "Hi there." Unfortunately her eyes had a will of their own and kept straying to Sam's baggy walking shorts. *No obvious bulge but that didn't mean it was all gone,* she told herself. Her overactive imagination had gone over every conceivable injury and had come to the conclusion that the damage must've been extensive.

Sam noticed the path of her eyes and felt a pang of regret narrow his own eyes. Saint Sali was every bit the procreating animal she'd been accused of. He looked at her strong arms and legs and wondered if she'd strangled Spencer or poisoned a batch of Holy Eggs. Maybe that was why she called them "Holy," he considered. Because they sent their victim to the Holy Land.

Sali drew her reluctant eyes from Sam's shorts to his face and saw the look of disgust there. Thinking he felt embarrassed to find her checking out his manliness or lack thereof, she grew flustered and her cheeks grew warm. She wet a hand with the hose and patted the cooling water on her cheeks. "It's going to be a hot one." Inside her brain screamed: Inane! Idiotic!

Sam leaned against the picket fence and looked at her appraisingly; she wore a loose, sleeveless cotton shirt over yet another pair of shapeless baggy shorts but he noticed that her legs were shapely. Her hair was windblown as usual, wild loops of dark curls that drifted over her shoulders. Sali watched his eyes rove over her body from head to toe and felt a warmth in her face that rapidly spread to her lower belly. "Did you have a nice walk?" she asked innocently, trying to tame her eyes' propensity to check him out in return.

"Yes, very nice."

"Well, I was just trying to get this yard under control..." Her voice tapered off, winding down as he didn't even pause in his perusal of her body, though his face was still shuttered with something that looked like disdain.

As soon as Sam had strode purposefully up his driveway and entered his house through the back door, Sali mentally stamped her foot at her own stupidity. He was probably very self-conscious about the injuries he had sustained in the explosion and her brazen examination of him hadn't helped. She shook her head to clear those thoughts and trudged up the steps to her own front door. The kids would be done with breakfast soon and the details of the day began to crowd her mind.

Sam stood very still in his kitchen. *She looked at my crotch!* he thought in indignant amazement. *No wonder those guys at the diner think I'm sleeping with her, if that's the way she looks at men.* On the heels of that thought came another, equally as shocking; she wouldn't be interested in looking if she knew I can't give her any more children.

A loud banging on his backdoor startled him out of his musings and peering through the curtained window he saw Bridget and Will standing there. Opening the door he found that they each clutched several sheets of brightly decorated paper. "We brung you pitures for your fridge!" Bridget announced loudly and Will smiled and nodded simultaneously.

"How nice! Let me see." The next half hour was taken up with providing lemonade and cookies for his guests while they explained in detail what each of the pictures represented and the convoluted stories they illustrated. By the time the pictures were hung on the refrigerator door with tape, since Sam didn't own any decorative magnets, another knock signaled Stephanie's arrival.

"Mama says it's time to come home." Turning to Sam she continued, "We're going to walk downtown and buy fireworks for Fourth of July." Sam was too surprised by her speaking more than just a few syllables to even notice what she had said.

"Fireworks!" Will started dancing around the kitchen. "I want loud bangs and pops!"

Bridget joined in the general revelry by spinning in a circle. "I'm a sparkler! I'm a sparkler!"

"Hey, hey" Sam chuckled as he put out a hand to stop her spinning before she crashed into something.

Bridget looked dizzily up at him, "Come with us, Mr. Tom Son! Fourth of July is only two days away and we need lots of fireworks."

Before he knew it Bridget's slightly sticky hand was on one side of him, and Will on the other and they were urging him toward the open kitchen door. Stephanie diplomatically stepped out of the way and once they had cleared the porch she carefully shut the door behind the group. Sali, standing in the back yard waiting for her missing children to show up, cringed as she saw Sam being forced forward. He smiled wryly at her and shrugged in resignation. "I'll get the garden cart."

As before, Bridget, Will and Jo rode in the garden cart pulled by Sam while Sali pushed Samuel in the stroller. This time, however, they were all much more casually dressed. Sam in his walking shorts and T-shirt, Sali in the same garb she had been wearing earlier during their conversation in the front yard, and the children in an odd collection of attire. Bridget was wearing a bathing suit top with cut off jeans on the bottom. Stephanie wore a summer dress with one strap pinned on with a duck-headed diaper pin while a pink flowered sunsuit strained over Jo's growing body. The boys were shirtless with elastic waisted shorts on their bottom halves, though baby Samuel had the added protection of a diaper. All of the children wore cheap rubber thongs on their feet.

Though it was still early in the day, the southern California sun made the air hot and the walk was less lively than it might have been. Sali found herself walking next to Sam, elbows bumping occasionally and they both companionably fielded questions and comments from the children.

The fireworks stand was set up in a temporary structure in the market parking lot and since the sun was nearly at its zenith there was no shade to speak of. Sali pulled a tiny cloth hat out of one of the ever present array of bags tucked in the cart and tied it onto the objecting baby to protect his head from the sun. By the time they walked away, Sam found he was the owner of the Family Size Fighting Tiger Fireworks Collection, a variety of assorted Bangs, Pops and Sparklers. Jo was given the important job of keeping the huge box from falling out of the cart as they jostled their way toward home.

Sali was inwardly cringing. She felt inordinately guilty for Sam's purchase of the fireworks when that hadn't been her intention at all. She decided a long talk with her children was in order to prevent them from manipulating him into any more extravagant shopping expeditions. But, she concluded, it was awfully nice of him to consider her kids in that way. She would never have spent that kind of money on fireworks, especially since she was now saving up the money to fix her car and the dryer.

"Hey, Mr. Tom Son..." Jo's face was the picture of innocence and he smiled at her in return, raising his eyebrows fractionally to invite her to go on. "Why don't you just get a wife so's you can have some babies?"

Sam felt his eyebrows shoot up even farther, it felt like all the way to his hairline. "What?"

"Now, Jo..." Sali began bravely. "Mr. Thompson may not want any babies and it really isn't any of our business if he has a wife!"

"But Mama, everybody wants babies and Mr. Tom Son doesn't have any!"

Sam was shocked into silence. Naturally, it was his conversation with Bridget about why he limped that had led to the revelation that he didn't have, nor probably never would have, any children of his own. He hadn't gone into detail, and thankfully she hadn't pushed for more information. Recovering from his surprise, he scrambled for an appropriate response. "Jo, why would I need a wife and babies when I have you kids living right next door to me, hanging pictures on my refrigerator and drinking my lemonade?" He smiled at his own cleverness.

"Okay! Hey everybody, we're gonna be Mr. Tom Son's kids now!" The children all cheered wildly, jostling one another and grinning at their great fortune.

Except for Albert. He hung back, keeping his serious face sober. He had seen the look on Mama's face when Jo made her announcement and knew that, much as the kids all loved Mr. Thompson, and much as Mr. Thompson maybe loved all of them, Mama and Mr. Thompson didn't love each other. And what good was a mother and father who didn't love each other? Albert had been through that with his Dad and wasn't about to open himself up for that kind of hurt again.

Sali groaned inwardly. "Oh, for heaven's sake!" she spat. "Really, Jo. There is more to being a father than hanging pictures on the fridge and drinking lemonade and Mr. Thompson knows that." They were almost back to the house and everyone sensed it was time to hold their tongues.

At the gate, Sam helped unload the kids, bags and fireworks from the garden cart, said a curt good-bye and then strode up his driveway. Sali watched him go and worried that his feelings were hurt because she hadn't been more enthusiastic about him being a surrogate father to her children.

The morning of the Fourth of July, was clear, muggy and hot. The town's Independence Day parade passed not far from Sali's street and it was a simple matter to walk her family half a block away, where they could sit on the curb and watch the rag tag parade march by.

The politicians passed first in borrowed convertibles, the mayor smiling broadly and his white-haired wife, looking only slightly wilted, waving at the citizens baking in the hot sun.

Then came the church floats; barely concealed religious themes and scenes set up on flatbed trucks. By the time the sports little leagues arrived, squirting the onlookers with high-powered squirt guns and spray bottles, Sali's kids were hungry, thirsty and tired. Samuel's eyes had long since drooped shut, and Sali pressed a kiss on his damp brow as she gathered up her brood.

Sam was coming down the street as the Kelley family were coming up from the parade. He waited for them to arrive and then asked, "Where have you all been?" Turning to Sali he said quietly, "You can borrow the garden cart any time you want."

"Oh, thanks but it was just a little ways. We went to watch the parade."

"I wish I'd known; I would have liked to have seen it." He watched her carefully to see if the kids' talk about his inability to have children, and their request that he take on the role of their father, had affected her in any way. The only thing he noticed was that she looked slightly flustered, but that might have been due to holding the rapidly growing Samuel, who was sleeping drooped and sweating over her shoulder.

"Ah, you didn't miss anything," Albert snarled and then stomped into the house. Sam raised an eyebrow in question at Sali but she merely shrugged in return.

"Don't feel bad." Bridget put her little browned and dusty hand on Sam's arm. "You can have hotdogs for lunch cause we always have hotdogs for lunch on Fourth-a-July! And come to the fireworks with us! And when it's the middle of the night we can do the bang pops you bought us!"

Again Sam looked at Sali, and again she shrugged, but this time she was smiling and he knew it was an invitation of sorts. "I would be honored to join your family for lunch, fireworks and bang pops," he countered in a serious voice. Though his comment was aimed at Bridget, he kept his eyes on Sali's face and was surprised to see color blossom on her smooth cheeks.

Sali turned up her walk, leaning back under the weight of her nephew, trying to control the foolish grin that threatened to erupt on her face. I must be crazy, she thought. I'm excited about a hot dog lunch with my neighbor.

Sam watched Sali walk toward her front door. She leaned back to counter-balance the weight of the baby, accentuating the curve of her back and the swell of her hips under the baggy shorts and ever-present t-shirt. Admiring her strong arms and shapely legs, he wondered how she managed to handle the kids, support them under what must be a huge financial burden and yet, still, smilingly cook up a Fourth of July hot dog lunch and plan a night of fireworks and celebration that would, undoubtedly, be designed for children and not for her own pleasure.

The kids had staked out a place in the municipal park that was open to the sky, covered in soft grass and fairly close to the fireworks launch pad. Sali spread a soft, old quilt on the turf and lay Samuel down. Sam leaned on one elbow, legs crossed at the ankles and watched her surreptitiously as she unpacked a bag of treats for the kids.

Around the group, families clustered in the gathering dusk, children slightly giddy with the novelty of being outside after dark and parents prepared to have a good time. A deep contentment settled over him and he considered that to any observer theirs was yet another family celebrating America's Independence Day with a day of food and fun behind them.

For lunch that day, Sam had created a fire in Sali's old, rusty barbecue, another relic rescued from City Dump. The kids had eaten their fill of burned hot dogs, gritty marshmallows and melting popsicles. Even Albert had loosened up enough to help Sam with the important and manly tasks of tending the fire and threading marshmallows onto straightened metal clothes hangers. Several lawn chairs and overturned crates had served as their furniture and after the simple meal Sam had enjoyed laying in a mildewed chaise lounge with Samuel curled up at his side napping.

The first explosion startled Sam from his thoughts, a red glittering starburst that blossomed overhead with a report that could be felt in his very bones. With a satisfied sigh of delight the children all stilled and looked expectantly toward the sky and for the next half hour there was no conversation. Sali had, at first, comforted Samuel who was distressed at the unusual noises and sights but soon his eyelids drooped and amazingly enough, he slept.

The finale was huge and lit up the entire area with zipping, sparkling and flashing things that shrieked and boomed and popped. A brief moment of absolute silence was followed by the murmur of the crowd talking and little bursts of applause. Sali gathered up her belongings while Sam folded the quilt and tucked it into the cart to pad the bottom for the kids' ride home.

"Can we do our fireworks now, Mr. Tom Son?" Bridget asked from her comfortable spot in the corner of the cart.

"Once we get home, honey." The endearment came naturally but shocked him just the same. He had never called anyone "honey" in his life and yet, there it was and his heart was filled with tenderness toward the small girl who had forced her way into his home, his life and his heart.

Sali felt her head jerk as Sam uttered the fatherly word of affection. At once her heart soared for her daughter to be so tenderly treated and then plummeted since it meant nothing, coming as it did, from a neighbor and not a father or even an uncle.

Her own brother had tried to fill the father role for her kids after Spencer had died but then, he too had died. How would her sons know how to be fathers themselves or her daughters know to recognize a good man without that element in their lives? Sali's father and mother lived on the other side of the country, and were in no position to be available and provide that input.

She briefly allowed herself a moment of fantasy, looking around at the tired group trudging home the short distance from the park. Breathing deeply of the damp night-scented air, Sali imagined herself married to Sam, going home with their children in tow. Knowing that after the last sparkler had fizzled they would curl up next to one another in bed and talk in quiet tones about the day, chuckling over some silly thing Bridget had done or some amazing observation that Albert had expressed. Sam would make a wonderful father but, she wondered, would he make a wonderful husband?

Never having considered herself an overtly sexual woman, she now considered the seriousness of being intimately involved with a man who was unable to express his masculinity in a physical way. How would she show him that she loved him? How would he do the same? Was physical love really that important? Not finding any answers she distracted herself by asking Albert about the constellations and then relaxed, enjoying a lively debate between her oldest son and Sam on the existence of extra-terrestrial beings.

Once at the house, Sam dragged a chair for Sali around to the front yard so that she could hold sleeping Samuel while the fireworks were ignited. Although he had suggested she lay the baby down inside he recognized the wisdom of keeping him with her because the noise might mask the sounds of his distress should he wake.

Further up the street other men were lighting fireworks under the excited and watchful eyes of their wives and children. Using the street as a safe and fireproof stage, Sam and Albert created a satisfying show of bangs and pops while Sali supervised sparklers in the hands of the younger children. When the last ember was out, she herded the kids inside for baths and bed while Sam carefully picked up every shred of paper, cardboard and confetti, dragging out the moment when the celebration was well and truly over and he would have to go home to his own house, surrounded by complete silence.

Chapter Five

ant a beer?" Sam's head shot up. Sali, barefoot and a little disheveled from dealing with the kids, stood a few feet away, in the dark of her front yard, holding two bottles of beer, condensation dripping from their sides.

"Sure. Sounds great." His voice was gruff and he cleared his throat self-consciously while reaching out for the brown bottle she offered. "Kids asleep?"

"Yeah. They were pooped out." Taking a swig off her bottle she looked up at the stars. "How about we sit in back and enjoy the quiet?"

Sali took the chaise lounger and stretched out with a moan of pleasure, shrugging the tension from her shoulders. Sam pulled a rocking lawn chair closer and kicking off his shoes, propped his feet up on the end of her chaise, near her crossed feet. The silence was comfortable and companionable but Sam found himself commenting, "Wasn't Bridget funny when she did that pirouette while holding the sparklers?"

Conversation washed over them, soft and warm and in waves like the gentle breakers on a fresh water lake. Sali turned a little on her side so that she could look at Sam while they talked and in the move found her foot brushing his. It felt good, and so she left it there and wondered if the slightly fuzzy feeling she was experiencing could be had from just one beer or was it the result of something else.

Sam idly moved his foot rhythmically against Sali's in time to the rocking of the chair and she felt the fuzzy feeling getting a shade warmer and settle in her lower belly making her body feel slow and languid.

They talked of Albert's knowledge of astronomy and his unwavering belief in aliens, as well as Stephanie's insecurity by being seemingly outshone by louder, wilder Bridget. They discussed Jo's recent growth spurt and Will's desire to be exactly like Albert. They marveled over Samuel's newest word, "wow" and his attempts at walking.

When their beers were gone Sam offered to fetch more from inside and while he was gone Sali looked up at the leafy branches overhead and considered that they were acting just like she had imagined in her fantasy earlier. The earthy smell of damp grass mingled with the distant, acrid scent of burning fireworks. Vaguely she was aware of the whine of bottle rockets on another street. Suddenly a cold, wet bottle being pressed against her cheek shocked her back to reality.

Sam had spent a moment in Sali's kitchen taking deep breaths and trying to talk himself out of his physical reaction, or over-reaction as the case may be, to Sali's nearness. That the touch of her foot and the sight of her neck where it met her shoulder could make him hot, was a revelation that he preferred to not dwell on. Better that he just get it under control. But the pulse beating below her jaw, even in the gloom of the back yard made his own pulse accelerate all over again and he had impulsively laid the cold beer bottle against her cheek. Her face, as it turned to him, was so open and soft and inviting the breath had caught in his throat.

Assuming the same position he had been in previously, only this time he deliberately found her foot with his and caressed it gently in time to the chairs rocking, Sam took a deep slug off the beer hoping to find some cooling relief.

Sali discovered that her foot had a life of its own as it returned Sam's caresses in what she prayed were insignificant movements.

"You asleep?" Sam was looking at her, eyes closed and head back with face to the sky as though it were a sunny day and the rays were warming her skin.

"No. Just thinking." Even her voice came out husky and raw and she took another swig off her beer only to discover that she had finished it. "I never did thank you properly."

"For what?" His eyes lit with amusement at what he took to be a slightly inebriated conversation.

"The box and the bath stuff. It was so nice of you. So thoughtful. I think of you every time I take a bath. I mean… oh, gee." She shook her head as though to shake away her embarrassment. *I just told him I think of him whenever I'm naked,* she groaned to herself.

Sam, recognizing her discomfort, reached out and laid a warm hand on her upper arm. "Sali, it's okay. I understand." Just then the whining of bottle rockets got louder and closer and erupted right next to Sali in a shower of sparks. Sam's hand tightened around her arm and pulled her towards him as she scrambled to the safety of his arms.

They stood there, between the two chairs, under the boughs of the shade tree, Sali trembling in delayed reaction. Sam's arms found their way around her shoulders and held her against his chest as she got herself under control. The small fire that had started as the result of the fireworks extinguished itself while another fire erupted within his body and began to burn out of control.

Sali felt Sam's arms tighten around her and she raised

her head questioningly to look at his face. His mouth descended in what he later told himself he had intended to be a comforting kiss not unlike what he would have bestowed upon Bridget, Stephanie or Jo in similar circumstances. The instant his warm lips touched hers, Sali felt the heat intensify and blossom in her belly. Her lips softened and molded to his. When he pulled away slightly her hand crept to his neck and pulled him closer.

Sam angled his body away from hers, trying to hide the betraying reaction of his lower body. Touching only with their faces, arms and hands they made a gentle exploration until he heard Sali's breath grow ragged, realizing his own was even more so, and pulled away. The expression on her face was one of hurt and loss and he pulled her back for one last kiss; a kiss that kindled the flames. Sali's lips nipped at his until he opened his mouth slightly and their tongues barely met in a soft gentle dance that tasted of beer and promises of more.

Sam purposefully set her away from him and cleared his throat. "I don't think there's any damage," he said looking toward the charred area of grass.

"What? Any damage? Of course not! It was just a kiss. For heaven's sake! Oh, it is late. I should really get inside." Sali knew her words were coming out choppy and stupid sounding but her only consolation was that she was in absolute shock. *No damage? Indeed! The gall of the man! How absolutely arrogant and typical!* She quickly gathered up the empty beer bottles and stomped toward the back door.

"Sali..."

Before she had time to react his hands grasped her upper arms and spun her around, pulling her tightly against him he slanted his mouth across hers and immediately kissed her deeply and passionately. His tongue entered her mouth and caressed the sensitive areas inside. Just as suddenly he thrust her from him and spun himself, hopping the picket fence and slamming into his own back door while Sali watched in utter amazement. From his back porch his disembodied voice floated back at her, "I was talking about the bottle rocket in the grass."

Pacing back and forth in his living room, Sam literally slammed his open palm against his forehead and muttered derogatory things about his own lack of intelligence. Was she Saint Sali or was she the husband killing, procreating beast that the men in the diner had described? Whichever, being in her arms had felt like heaven.

Sali curled up on her side in bed, crying for her own stupidity. How could she have thrown herself at her neighbor? She had to live next door to him and the children liked him and now she had gone and confused the whole situation. He was probably bored while she was attacking him like that, since the accident had blown off his male packaging. It hadn't gone unnoticed by her that he had held himself away from her, trying to hide his lack of arousal from her as she had shamelessly pressed her body against him. Groaning in despair she finally fell into a troubled sleep just as the summer sun was glowing in the east.

The children, well-rested unlike their mother, were talkative during breakfast in the sunny kitchen. Sali woodenly answered their questions, dished up bowls of cold cereal and made excessive but satisfying noise by clanging dishes around. Soon even talkative Bridget grew silent watching Sali agitatedly wash the dishes. "I think I'll go say hi to Mr. Tom Son," the child said quietly.

Sali spun around wild-eyed. "No!" All of the kids looked at her in shock. "I mean, Mr. Thompson is probably busy doing things. And, you really shouldn't go and bug him." She hid her face from them and went back to washing dishes while the kids filed out.

As soon as Albert was sure that the others were busy he sidled around to the front of the house. Snoopy little Bridget had waylaid the other girls to be her slaves in a game of Cleopatra in the back yard. Will was zooming cars around the living room floor and Samuel was watching in goofy baby delight. Mama was sitting in her flowered chair staring blankly at a magazine on her lap. It was safe to perform his mission without being followed.

Albert quickly opened his gate and walked purposefully to Sam's house next door. He rang the bell and waited, fidgeting for fear someone would spot him. Mama's swollen, tear stained eyes hadn't gone unnoticed by Albert and as the man of the house it was his duty to have a talk with Sam

Sam heard the doorbell from his place at the kitchen table. Bringing his mug of coffee with him he padded barefoot to the front door. If he was surprised to see Albert, Albert was doubly surprised to see Sam, shirtless and shoeless, unshaven and looking just as unhappy as Mama.

"I need to talk to you." Albert kept his eyes on the mug in Sam's hand while he spoke, feeling that in some way it would be violation of Sam's privacy to look him in the eye.

Sam opened the door wider and motioned with the mug for Albert to come in. Wordlessly and by mutual unspoken consent they filed through to the kitchen, sitting at the chrome and black lacquer table.

"I need to talk to you," Albert repeated. "My mom is pretty upset this morning."

Sam could see that this conversation was costing Albert plenty in the courage department. He briefly considered that Sali might have sent the boy over to plot her next move in the planned seduction and murder of her neighbor. "Go for it," he said crisply.

"Well, my mom is over at our house trying not to cry."

Sam started to rise from his chair in an unconscious effort to go to her and render comfort. Realizing the futility of that action he sat back heavily. "And do you think I have something to do with that?"

"She never usually cries except when the kids do something mean to her. Or like when Dad died or when Uncle Joe and Aunt Miranda died. So I figure something has hurt her bad."

"What does all of this have to do with me?" Sam took a gulp of his coffee, discovered it to be cold and managed to swallow it without gagging.

"It all started when Bridget told us that you couldn't have kids and that you wanted us for your kids. That means you want Mama for your wife. But Mama has been hurt enough. My dad made her cry all the time and I don't think she needs another husband. Besides, I take care of the little kids. We don't need a dad." Albert took a shaky breath, feeling his face flush with the effort this conversation was costing him. "If you really want a kid of your own you can get one the same way we got Samuel."

Sam held his breath, intuitively recognizing that a mystery was about to be solved. "How did you get Samuel?"

"Uncle Joe and Aunt Miranda died and in their will they said we got Samuel so we took him home. He was way little then and he won't even remember them. Mama said we have to remember them for him so's he can know all about them."

"You adopted him?" Sam felt equal measures of guilt for his suspicions about Sali's moral fiber and relief that he had been wrong.

"No, we don't need to. Uncle Joe was Mama's brother so she's Samuel's guardian now. She says he doesn't need to be adopted because he still has parents. In heaven." The last words were spoken quietly though with great emotion and Sam recognized that Albert's grief was still fresh.

Gently, Sam spoke, "and how long ago was that, that they died?"

"Well, Samuel is ten months old now and they died when he was three months old so it was ten take away three... that's seven months ago."

Seven months ago. Seven months ago Sali had taken in her orphaned nephew and fit him right into her already over large and overburdened household. His respect for her grew. "How long ago did your dad die, Albert?"

"When I was 7. Two years ago."

The solemn voice spoke volumes and Sam was quiet knowing that there were no words that would offer the sort of comfort a boy needs in the face of the loss of his father.

"Anyway, you can just tell people that if they die you'll take their kids and then you can have kids of your own. People die all the time." Albert's own experiences had proven that observation. He took a deep breath that shuddered a little at the height of it. "You don't need us and my Mama doesn't need you."

Sam was momentarily struck dumb. He recognized that a denial of wanting the kids would be a rejection of sorts but to say that he did want them would prove Albert's theory that Sam and Sali were headed toward marital discord.

"Albert," Sam began raking his fingers through his already messy hair causing it to stand up on end. "I like you kids a lot. And I like your mom a lot. But it takes more than just liking someone to consider marrying them. Your mom and I don't go on dates. We don't like each other that way." Briefly considering the sizzling kiss of the night before, Sam felt a moment's unease as though he was telling an untruth.

Albert was shaking his head. "I don't know about that.

If you want us kids it just makes sense that if you're going to be the dad and my mom is the mom that you two would get married. But we don't need a dad bad enough to hurt my mom."

"Why do you think she's crying? How do you think I've hurt her?" Sam asked.

"I think she's just sad. She was always sad when my dad was alive."

Sali looked up from her inner thoughts and saw that Will had abandoned his game and Samuel was getting cranky. She swept him into her arms and blew bubbles on his round belly making him chuckle like a stream running over smooth rocks. Looking out the kitchen window she could see the girls paying homage to Bridget, fanning her with a hollyhock leaf and acting out her fantasies. Sali smiled, wondering how that little scrap of future woman-hood could manage to get everyone to do her bidding. The world was in for trouble once Bridget grew up, that was for sure. Will had made himself a peanut butter and jelly sand-wich and left the gooey knife on the counter. Sitting on the back steps he was alternately taking a bite and offer-ing it to a neighborhood cat that sat, tail twitching, nearby.

Albert walked in the front door and went straight to his room, body language screaming, "leave me alone" and Sali, sensitive to her oldest child's moods, did just that.

"Hey Will," she called out the window. He looked up at her, and seeing her brow was once again serene and her eyes had lost that hurt look he smiled. "Let's make ice cream!" Sali called out and the girls dropped the hollyhock leaves and Bridget bounced up and took off at a run. Mama was okay and all was, once again, right with their world.

Sam noticed in the following days that if he stepped outside onto his back porch while Sali was in her back yard she scurried inside. At first he humored her and looked outside before opening the door, not wanting to add to her distress but as the days went by he decided since they were living next door to one another they had to resolve the problem. Deciding that the first step would be to let Albert in on what he was planning, so as not to add to the boy's distress. Enlisting his support would be easy since after their talk the boy seemed much more willing to be friends.

"Albert, can I talk to you a minute?" Sam called across the fence. Albert was going through a stash of alley finds which looked like an old record player, part of a lawn mower and some scraps of plywood. He leapt up and trotted to the fence which separated the yards. In the middle of summer the lawns had turned brittle and the flowers were seedy and leggy looking. The deep shade of the old elm still held a restful appeal, and the buzz of cicadas indicated that others besides Sam found it attractive.

Sam explained quickly that his plan was to make friends with Sali once again and Albert readily agreed to help. "No romance stuff," he warned. Their business concluded, Sam asked what Albert was going to do with his trash day haul. "I'm going to build something. I haven't decided yet what it will be."

"If you need any help just let me know."

The next morning was Sunday, and though Sam hadn't noticed Sali taking the kids to church lately he carefully showered, shaved and dressed in a white shirt and slacks. Dusting off the garden cart he lined it with a blanket and then pulled it around to the front. He swallowed once or twice before knocking on Sali's door.

Sali's shock was evident on her face when she opened the door and found Sam, black hair gleaming damply, face smooth, and trim slacks accentuating the fitness of his lower body, standing on her doorstep. "Hi," he said brightly. "Want a ride to church?"

The kids were ready in record time, and in the privacy of her bedroom Sali nervously pulled a polyester dress over her underwear. Its simple style skimmed her figure, a noticeably thinner figure since the Fourth of July. She ran a brush through her riotous curls and spritzed herself with a summer fragrance. Sam was waiting in the living room, sitting in her flowered chair, with kids leaning on him smiling. Even Albert was pleased and baby Samuel seemed excessively thrilled to be balanced on one of Sam's sinewy thighs.

Sali's tongue seemed stuck. She couldn't think of a thing to say. Here she was, walking to church with Sam and all she could think about was how good it had felt to be held in his arms the night he had kissed her.

What was the meaning of his invitation to church? she wondered. Braving a sideways glance at him she noticed he looked quite self-satisfied. He was listening attentively to Albert who was uncharacteristically animated in a discussion about what to do with a bunch of junk he'd found in the garbage. They were debating the merits of using a turntable motor and lawnmower wheels versus a lawnmower motor and roller-skate wheels for some contraption of indeterminate use.

"If you use the lawnmower motor and the lawnmower wheels but make a new frame..."

"I want something new, though. Not just a lawnmower with a platform!"

"Okay, how about we get some PVC pipe and..."

Sali tuned them out. It was all Greek to her anyway and here she was worrying about having to say something. They were lost in their own world of guy talk. Her heart missed a beat and she actually stopped, causing Stephanie to run into her and Samuel to look back and see what the hold up was. Sam raised his eyebrows but he and Albert continued uninterrupted.

She had been so selfish, thinking only of her own needs and desires. Her kids did need a dad and who better than someone who wouldn't be out chasing skirts in bars. A man who, because of a tragic accident, was incapable to cheating on her. Suddenly it was all clear. Sam needed kids and her kids needed Sam. It didn't matter what she needed and if she were very careful she wouldn't let it bother her that some of those needs would never be met.

"We're here." Sam's voice cut into her revelation and she looked up to see the churchyard filled with milling people.

This time the parishioners were ready for the unusual sight of Sali accompanied by a man. They took it in stride, and some even managed to greet Sam as though he was an old friend including Mrs. Browning who smiled in greeting just as the opening hymn started.

Sam had chosen to sit at the far end of the pew so that all of the kids were between he and Sali. He figured he'd keep an eye on them from one end and she could manage from the other. The time came for Sunday School and after the older kids had all filed out he gratefully scooted down next to her. She nervously smoothed her skirt where Samuel had bunched it up but when he squealed loudly during a prayer Sam wordlessly took him and stepped outside with the bored baby.

The sun was hot but a slight breeze kept it from being stifling. Sam bounced Samuel about and told him nonsensical things about the trees and the wind and what might be on the menu for lunch. Sam kept talking even as the baby lay his head down on the strong shoulder offered and fell asleep. Mumbling softly, gentle words to keep the baby sleeping, Sam slipped back inside and into the pew next to Sali. She raised her eyebrows in question and Sam mouthed back that Samuel had fallen asleep.

For the rest of the service Sam held the sleeping baby and Sali knew she should enjoy this moment of relative peace. It wasn't often that the children weren't her sole responsibility and the novelty of having someone share that role was hard for her to accept.

As though there was a magnet in her body and her brain, Sali's entire being was focused on Sam's still form next to her on the hard bench. Samuel was draped across the man's chest and shoulder, snoring slightly with a glistening spot of drool forming a wet spot on the immaculate shirt under his rosebud mouth.

Discovering she was even leaning in Sam's direction, drawn to him like some demented moth to a flame, she pulled herself suddenly and sharply upright.

Sam saw Sali's sudden movement out of the corner of her eye and turned to see her blushing. He wondered if she had fallen asleep and then jerked awake. He raised his eyebrows in question at her rosy cheeks. Blushing deeper, the heat spreading to her ears and chest, Sali looked earnestly at the hymnal in her lap.

After church Sam dawdled, keeping hold of Samuel so that Sali couldn't slip away. He spoke to the Pastor, Mrs. Browning and several other people while Sali stood by nervously watching. The older kids darted here and there, finding friends in amongst the family groups on the churchyard and Sam kept talking until Sali thought she'd scream with frustration. Mrs. Browning tapped her on the shoulder startling her to such a degree that she let out a little shriek.

"Oh, dear. I am so sorry I frightened you. You have quite a friend in that Sam Thompson, dear. He's holding your nephew like he was his own child and the other children seem quite taken with him, also."

Sali smiled and nodded and made some inane excuse to go to Sam's side. "Are you about ready to go?" she whispered.

Sam smiled to himself. Those were the first words she had uttered directly to him since the Fourth of July. "Anytime you want, Sali."

Something about the way he said her name sent shivers up her spine. It seemed so intimate and yet, how could that be, she wondered. The man couldn't be intimate. At least, not the sort of intimacy his deep voice seemed to promise when he said her name.

Calling the children together, Sali took the sleeping baby from Sam, her breast brushing his arm in the process, strapped him into the stroller, said good-bye to those around her, but all the time aware of the decision she had made. Sam would make a good father and since her goal was to provide everything her kids needed she would provide them with Sam. It might take awhile but she would do it. And, she decided, she would never, ever let him know that she regretted the loss of the physical side of love.

Sam noticed Sali's body language change as soon as she took the baby. While he lifted each of the younger children into the garden cart he was aware of Sali offering comfort to him simply by standing at his elbow saying good-bye to the other churchgoers.

That was it! he realized. She was standing at his elbow in a comfortable way that spoke volumes. As though she was intimately familiar with him and had every right to be so near, so possessive, she invaded his body space.

The quick brush of her full breast hadn't gone unnoticed, either. Though he would have liked to believe it was a deliberate action, he knew it had to be accidental. Those brief kisses they had shared the other night had sent her into such a tizzy he couldn't imagine her doing something as blatant as rubbing up against him. But it had felt nice, just the same. Better than nice he decided, as his body thickened in response.

"Are you gonna have lunch with us again?" Bridget asked quietly. It seemed that none of the children had a clue how to react to the mixed signals being sent round them by the grown-ups in their lives.

"If your mother invites me, I will."

Sali smiled. "Sam, would you like to have lunch with us today?" she asked primly.

"Yes, thank you." The unusually polite tones were at odds with normal life with this crew and Sam was wary. *Was she already plotting to kill him*, he wondered. Maybe this new physical closeness was her way of seducing him into letting down his guard.

Why was he trying to make friends with her? He asked himself. *What the hell was wrong with him?* Shaking his head to ward off his confusion he settled his arm around Albert's thin shoulders.

Lunch was a roast that Sali had started early that morning, along with tender potatoes, carrots and celery. Fluffy rice, homemade gravy and the ever-present summer zucchini rounded out the meal. For desert Sam pulled a gallon of ice cream from his freezer and dressed it up with strawberries from his garden that he asked the girls to pick. Conversation was relaxed and mainly centered on the children but Sali noticed an undercurrent of some other element that she couldn't identify.

Her fingers lightly touched Sam's as she handed him the bowl of strawberries, but he seemed oblivious. It had been many years since Sali had played the flirting game but surely she remembered that Spencer had responded to such slight overtures such as that. Sam's hands were rock steady and her touch had no effect on him. Drawing back, she recognized what she felt as a sense of hurt and insecurity

Sam was baffled by the mixed messages Sali was sending. Her hand brushed his as she passed the bowl of berries to him but moments later when she offered him more ice tea she was careful to avoid any contact whatsoever. She even seemed to have a slight tremble to her fingers and her face was alternately flushed and pale.

In spite of her decision to obtain Sam for her children, she grew flustered. Maybe he didn't like her at all. Maybe he only put up with her so he could be around the kids. She felt so hopelessly maternal it seemed absurd to think that she could attract him. As her thoughts whirled around 360 degrees, she remembered that the goal wasn't to attract him to her, but to her kids. Putting a hand to her head she gazed unseeingly at the bowl of ice cream in front of her.

"Are you okay, Sali?" Sam asked, having noticed her sudden pallor and apparent weakness. *What if something happened to her*, he wondered in horror. Who would take her children as she had taken her brother's child? No one could be a better mother than she to this strange group of amazingly diverse personalities. What if someone wanted to split them all up? What would he, Sam, do if he didn't have Sali and this brood in his life?

Sali watched Sam's face darken with concern. "I'm okay, Sam. Just a little too much sun and not enough sleep I guess." She suddenly jumped up and started clearing plates away. For all that she moved with energy, Sam detected some sort of sorrow in the slump of her shoulders and the tiny worry line between her eyebrows deepened.

Chapter Six

The jangling of the phone brought Sali in from the backyard at a run. She had been hanging laundry while Samuel played at her feet in the tall grass. The other kids were scattered here and there; Stephanie, sitting in the shade of the old elm tree, was completely absorbed in her latest *Babysitters Club* book. Albert was tinkering with some mechanical monstrosity he was building, Bridget and Jo were playing Barbie dolls in the once again stagnant water of the pond and Will quietly driving matchbook cars along the stone wall at the back of the property.

"Hello," Sali gasped breathlessly as she grabbed up the phone on its fourth ring.

The familiar voice of Sali's friend from one street over, Tracy Greene, greeted her laughingly. "What are you doing? You sound like you can hardly breathe."

"I ran in from outside. I was hanging laundry because the dryer broke."

Tracy, a short blonde with a spunky attitude, shook her head in horror. "Hanging laundry with the amount of washing you have to do with that crew? You poor thing! You can come use my dryer if you want."

Sali laughed at Tracy's words. "It's not so bad. I just

think of it as a Solar Dryer." Holding the phone between one shoulder and her cheek she began wiping the counter and putting dry dishes away in cupboard. "To what do I owe the great honor of your call?"

"Well, we're going to have a *Dog Days of Summer* picnic and bake sale. You might have read about it in the Church Bulletin."

Sali's looked over at the overflowing mail basket that she hadn't had time to go through lately and saw the newsletter peeking out from between a couple of advertisements. "No, I didn't notice..." she said weakly.

"Uh, huh. Still haven't gone through your mail, right? Anyway, I'm looking for volunteers to make cookies and pies for the bake sale. Do you think you're up to the task?" Tracy was one of the few people who seemed to respect, if not fully understand, how much energy and time it took to mother 6 kids.

"It would be my pleasure. What's the money for?" The dishes put away, Sali moved on to straightening jars in the spice cabinet.

Tracy explained that the proceeds would go into the Family Assistance fund for needy families during the holidays. She didn't need to remind Sali that there had been plenty of times that Spencer had partied away his paycheck and Sali herself was the recipient of the fund. In fact, if it hadn't been for the generosity of her church, one Christmas the children would have had a barren holiday.

The two women discussed and agreed upon the items Sali would donate, promising to seek each other out at the picnic the following Saturday.

"Oh, Sali," Tracy added. "Before I forget. Be sure and invite your friend."

Sali's mind went blank. *Her friend?* "Who?"

Tracy chuckled. "You know. The man you're seeing. Bring him! See you." The connection severed, Sali stared at the handset as though it were a snake. Tracy thought she was dating Sam. "Oh, God," she muttered to herself.

Mortification warred with semi-hysteria until Sali realized it was all playing right into her plan. *Sam for her kids*, she mentally chanted as she went through her files for cookie and pie recipes.

It didn't take long for Sali to go through the cupboards, decide what she needed from the store, and write out a list. Steeling her courage she brushed her hair, slipped on sandals and walked next door.

Sam was at the computer researching a company he was thinking of buying stock in when he heard the doorbell. Absent mindedly cleaning his glasses on a tissue he opened the door and squinted in confusion at Sali standing on his front porch.

"Hi!" she said brightly. And then was struck dumb at the sight of him. He was wearing loose walking shorts, slung low across his hips. Though he wore a faded blue shirt it was unbuttoned exposing his lightly furred chest. Rolled up at the sleeves, every movement of his fingers rubbing the tissue across the lens of his glasses made the muscles move in his forearms.

Sam quickly replaced his glasses on his nose and blinked at Sali. "Is something wrong?" he asked. The look on her face was one he hadn't seen before and he couldn't really tell what it meant.

Running her tongue across suddenly dry lips, Sali cleared her throat. "I was hoping I could borrow your wagon. I need some things from the store."

"I think I'll come along, if you don't mind. I need a break from the computer. I've been staring at it too long," Sam said as he buttoned up his shirt. Sali dragged her eyes away from his chest and shrugged her shoulders, as if to say it didn't matter to her one way or the other but the skin of her back tingled in awareness as she turned to leave with Sam following.

To carry the groceries on the way back, Albert pulled Sali's small, rusty red wagon. Stephanie pushed Samuel in the stroller and Sam pulled the large cart with the three younger kids riding high in style. Sali, for a change, had her hands free.

As she listened to Sam talk with the kids she realized that during the long, hot summer they had been forging friendships. They talked, joked and made reference to other conversations. She felt a little left out at the thought that they had common memories and experiences that didn't include her. Mentally kicking herself, she remembered her goal: Sam for her kids.

Sam glanced over at Sali who was walking by herself, clutching her sack of a purse as though it were a lifeline. She looked as though she hadn't a friend in the world and for once Sam gave in to his urge to touch her. Reaching out with his free hand he grabbed hers and pulled her up next to him.

Sali found herself telling him about the Family Assistance Fund, and the coming picnic with the kids adding in their expectations and memories of past church gatherings. "Would you like to join us, Sam?" she asked shyly, unbelievably aware of the feel of his large warm hand holding hers.

"When I was about eight I had a friend who would invite me to his family picnics. Once, we ended up having a food fight. Even his parents got into the act and threw hot dog buns and marshmallows." Sam grinned in remembrance of that silly time. "I'd love to go to a picnic." He realized that her hand was still firmly ensconced within his and gave her fingers a little squeeze.

"I wanna have a food fight!" Bridget exclaimed. Sali shook her head in warning at Sam before he could promise to fulfill that particular fantasy.

Sam's eyes met Sali's over the brown-haired heads surrounding them at elbow height. Somehow he knew the exact message she was sending him and winked at her to show he understood. He wouldn't promise or encourage any food fights at the picnic. He saw the corners of her mouth twitch in an unrepentant grin before she quickly turned her head away.

At the store they quickly went through Sali's grocery list choosing tart apples for pie, and chocolate chips and walnuts for cookies. Sam picked out thinly sliced ham, swiss cheese and crusty rolls. At Jo's request he added the biggest jar of kosher dill pickles the store carried. At the last minute he grabbed a box of popsicles. Packing the smaller cart full of their purchases they headed home, each with a popsicle to enjoy on the hot walk.

Sali put Sam and Albert to the task of peeling apples on the back steps while she rolled out pie crust. Jo happily poured pre-measured sugars and spices into a huge crockery bowl while Bridget hung curling strips of apple peel over her fingers, teasing Samuel until he grabbed them, chuckling happily. Stephanie sat at the big oak table "researching" cookie recipes, trying to decide which would be the best to make.

Finally the pies were in the oven. Sali put Jo and the baby into the bathtub to clean the sticky apple juices and sugars off their hands and faces. Sam turned the sprinklers on in the yard and the older kids frolicked in water while the sun slowly set. The scent of apples and spices permeated the sultry summer air.

Sam sat in one of the disreputable lawn chairs watching the kids and thought about Sali inside, puttering about in the kitchen. Every once in awhile he heard the kitchen sink go on, a pan clatter on the stove or the silly shriek of the baby in the tub.

Though he had never had a family like this, he recognized that this was what he had been looking for all his life. This sense of belonging and unity. Even when the kids acted up, or a disaster struck, like when Jo accidentally poured a second teaspoon of salt into the pie filling, no one was made to feel like they didn't measure up. He knew that this sense of rightness and acceptance was Sali's doing.

Though he was tempted to hang around longer he didn't want to wear out his welcome. Bridget barreled her wet body against his as he said his good-byes and hugged him tightly. He found himself kissing the top of her head and as he raised his eyes saw that Sali was watching closely. He winked at her and was shocked when she winked back.

Sali watched Sam vault the fence between their yards and disappear into the gloom of the rapidly falling darkness. She had intended asking him to dinner but had hesitated, ashamed to expect him to share their simple meal of fish sticks and french fries. What with making pies all afternoon and bathing the little kids she just didn't have time or energy to make anything elaborate.

The rest of the week was spent mixing and baking numerous batches of cookies until by the day of the Dog Days of Summer Bake Sale and Picnic Sali had managed to box up about 8 dozen. There had been more but with 6 kids and Sam sampling them, several dozen were consumed.

Tracy was good enough to offer to drive several kids and the goodies to the picnic in her min-van. Bridget, Stephanie and Jo gladly joined Tracy's own 4 kids inside the bright blue vehicle, leaving Sali with just the boys. Sam had already volunteered to drive them. He sauntered over just as Tracy slammed the back doors shut on the van.

"You must be Sam," Tracy said happily thrusting out her hand. "I'm Tracy Greene, the one responsible for blackmailing Sali into baking all week."

Sam looked at the bouncy blonde, who was diminutive enough that she could be one of the kids and smiled. Shaking her hand he laughingly said, "Believe me, it was the kids' and my pleasure! We got to sample everything."

Tracy turned to Sali, who was standing nearby watching the exchange, and grinned. In a stage whisper she added, "He's a keeper," as she jumped into the driver's seat. Chuckling, Sam slapped the window as the van moved away from the curb, to the sound of the three Kelley girls calling good-bye.

The boys fit into the back seat of Sam's car with plenty of room, even with the baby's car seat. Sali belted herself in and then ran her hand over the creamy leather upholstery. The desire for luxurious things had never been one of her faults, but she could see how someone would enjoy, want and even covet a nice car like Sam's complete with power windows, air conditioning and leather seats. She sighed, wondering why all of a sudden just surviving wasn't good enough.

For so long Sali had been in survival mode. Paying bills, buying groceries and the odd treat here and there had satisfied her. To sleep through the night, with Samuel's cooperation, to get through a meal without a major spill, to kiss her children goodnight without a tearful tale of some wrongdoing during the day, had been the goal. Now, she realized that she was living life in reverse. Expecting the worst, being thrilled by the absence of bad, she no longer even knew what good things she could covet.

"Ready?" Sam questioned, interrupting her thoughts,

knowing that she was adamant about not driving until the kids were all belted in.

"Onward!" she exclaimed.

During the drive Albert questioned Sam about the power windows, and power seat controls, and the likelihood of finding similar devices in the City Dump and there started a lively conversation about what sorts of interesting inventions he could create if only he had the "right parts." Sali stifled a gasp as her wayward mind mocked her own desires about Sam's "parts."

The large expanse of rolling hills covered with mown grass and interspersed with trees, shrubs and the local Hoe and Grow Garden Club's flowering beds had attracted record numbers of picnickers. A small man-made pond filled with darting goldfish sparkled in the hot sunshine and brightly colored quilts dotted the grounds to mark each family's territory.

Sali spotted the Bake Sale tables and found that her contributions had already been placed amongst the other offerings. She was glad to see that her pies looked as good as any and her cookies were already being purchased to add to picnic lunches. Tracy, with the skill of a drill sergeant, was directing kids to drag chairs and tables, tie awning ropes and generally keep moving in a helpful manner.

Sam, carrying Samuel and the ever-present bags, along with two large piece-work quilts set off across the grass looking for a shady place to stake out as their own. Albert followed dragging an ice chest on wheels filled with frosty lemonade and potato salad. Will brought up the rear with the picnic basket itself. He had peeked inside and knew that Sam had made ham and cheese as well as some peanut butter and jelly sandwiches, the boys' personal favorite.

"How's this, boys?" Sam asked his entourage at one nicely sized shady area that looked as though it would stay in the shadow of a tree throughout the afternoon. With a groan, Albert gave his approval by collapsing onto the thick, soft grass and rubbing his thin biceps to demonstrate just how tough it had been to drag the heavy ice chest.

On the other side of the park Sali shaded her eyes and looked across the green expanse. She had gathered up her girls after Tracy was done with them but now she was having trouble locating Sam and the boys. Finally she spotted a tall man holding a laughing baby in the air and realized that it was Sam and his namesake.

For some reason her heart gave a little lurch when she saw Sam and the boys from across the park. It was as though, from a distance she could see him clearer than she could up close. Her senses weren't blinded by the energy his body seemed to communicate to hers whenever they were in close proximity.

He was thin, but not as thin as he had been at the beginning of summer, she noticed. His muscles had filled out from all of his walking. His hair had been left to get a little longer than she imagined he usually allowed it, with a slight flip starting at the base of his neck. The loose shorts he was wearing, rather than looking baggy and concealing, looked like what they were, expensive name brand walking shorts such as several other fit fathers were wearing in the park that day. The T-shirt stretched tight across his shoulders displayed well-defined muscles playing across his bones with the effort of holding the chunky baby in the air.

Licking her lips, Sali slowed her pace across the park, even as the girls sped up and raced toward the others. *How could she have missed this?*, Sali wondered. Just the sight of him was a turn-on. As though he had picked up her thoughts he turned toward her, and a smile of pleasure and welcome spread across his face. And something else, too that made Sali's heartbeat faster and heat blossom in her cheeks.

"Just my luck," she muttered to herself, "to discover I have hormones when I've made up my mind not to use them."

Sam heard the girls' whooping laughter before he actually saw them. They raced across the park toward him and following slowly behind was Sali. She had an odd look on her face, like she was confused. Taking another moment to twirl the baby around in the air again, making him laugh his throaty little chuckle, Sam spared her another glance.

A slight breeze was fluttering Sali's wild curls around her shoulders. The same breeze had flattened her too-large T-shirt against her body showing that her figure underneath was slender, though full-busted. With a will of their own, his eyes were drawn to the movement of that full bust as she walked toward him. Just enough of a bounce for him to be mesmerized, he hoped no one else was noticing that enticing jiggle.

Her muscular legs were well-defined beneath the drawstring shorts that fluttered about her hips. All in all, she was a beautiful woman and he wondered why she hid behind all that loose cloth. Standing in the park, surrounded by the kids who were rolling, laughing and crawling around him on the quilts, and watching Sali approaching, suddenly gave him a enormous sense of well-being and belonging. *If only these could be his kids and that could be his woman,* he thought in shock, he would be a happy man.

Various activities were held throughout the afternoon including a sack race that Bridget somehow talked Sali and Sam into entering. Feeling awkward, they slid the rough burlap sack over their adjacent legs. Trying to walk, however, proved quite difficult until Sam stopped Sali, "Here, like this," he said slipping his arm around her shoulders. She wrapped her arm around his trim waist and they took a few experimental steps. Although that made it easier to walk in sync, the smooth skin on Sali's leg rubbing against the hair-roughened musculature of Sam's appendage felt like fire.

Taking their place at the starting line Sam sized up their opponents. Pastor and Mrs. Morris, plump and out of shape, Tracy and Bob, her husband and male counterpart matching her in size and energy, and several other people he recognized from church. He gave Sali's shoulders a squeeze as the final countdown began. "On your marks, get set... GO!"

Sali struggled to keep pace with Sam's movements as they hopped, ran and skipped toward the finish line to the sound of cheers from the kids. Glancing quickly to the sidelines she saw Albert holding Samuel on his thin hip, uncharacteristically animated as he spurred them on with shouts of "Go, Mama! Go, Sam!"

The moment's distraction was enough for her to lose her rhythm and she felt her feet become tangled in Sam's. Down they went in a jumble of arms and legs, ending up with one feminine thigh wrapped around Sam's hip. His knee was pressed intimately against the juncture of her own thighs bringing a wave of heat.

Sam laughed breathlessly as he quickly drew his offending appendage away from her body. It took a moment to get all their parts sorted out giving the other racers the edge they needed to get ahead. Sali and Sam were barely standing when Tracy and Bob crossed the finish line to be declared the winners.

Amid pats on the back and shouted greetings the contestants all stumbled back to their respective picnic spots where everyone ate far too much and grew lazy in the summer afternoon heat.

Sam lay dozing in the shade with Samuel curled up snoring softly next to him. The shouts and laughter of children in the distance were a pleasant background noise to fall asleep to and Sali sat cross-legged on the quilt next to them trying to avoid the lure of a lazy afternoon's nap.

Tracy trotted up and quietly motioned for Sali to follow her. She rose gracefully from her spot beside Sam to retreat to the shade of an adjacent tree. "So, how's it going," Tracy asked with a knowing grin.

"Okay. We've had a great time today." Sali was perplexed at the avid curiosity displayed on her friend's face.

"C'mon, Sali... give. Sam seems so nice and he genuinely likes the kids. How serious are you two?" Tracy had all the subtlety of a steamroller but she had often bragged that that was how she found out so much about what was going on around her.

"He's just a friend!" Sali whispered fiercely. "Hold your voice down! I don't want him to know we're having this conversation."

"Just a friend, my Aunt Fanny. He looks at you and your kids like he's hungry and you're what it will take to satisfy him."

"Please, Tracy. I can't believe you're saying this stuff. There is nothing romantic going on at all." Sali glanced furtively at Sam and Samuel's sleeping forms, breathing a sigh of relief when she saw that they hadn't moved.

Sam kept his eyes shut and concentrated on keeping his breathing deep and even. The women's words had worked into his drowsing brain and brought him to the surface of consciousness. They were far enough away that he didn't catch all the words, there was too much background noise for that, but he heard enough to know that Tracy, the little powerhouse, was grilling Sali on the nature of their relationship. He felt his lips twitch and fought against the grin that was threatening to erupt on his face.

"I know when a man is interested in a woman and believe me, Sam wants to be more than friends!" Amusement laced the shorter woman's voice at Sali's discomfiture.

Sam was startled to hear that he was attracted to Sali but it made sense and he managed to control the flicker of his eyelids, keeping up his pretense of being asleep.

"Tracy, I am telling you, Sam and I are just friends and besides," Sali's voice had risen just a notch and there was a little catch in her throat, "if he wanted a girlfriend he sure wouldn't pick a woman saddled with six kids and a boring life!"

Sali couldn't admit her plan to Tracy. If it failed she'd be humiliated when everyone found out she had been rejected.

Sam winced inwardly. Is that how she saw herself? She didn't act like she felt "saddled" and her life was anything but boring. The kids made sure of that.

"I cook, clean, sing lullabies and wipe runny noses all day. For heaven's sake, I don't even have time to watch TV or read the paper and the last book I read was a romance novel. I couldn't have an intelligent conversation if my life depended on it." She paused to catch her breath, finding she was on the verge of a sob.

"Don't be ridiculous!" Tracy hissed. "Any man worth his salt would be proud to be involved with you and your kids. And unless I miss my guess, Sam Thompson is worth his salt."

Sali just shook her head, fighting the lump in her throat and the stinging in her nose, heralding the threat of tears.

"Do you know what your problem is, Sali?" At Sali's

shake of her head, Tracy continued, though she would have probably continued in any case. " Spencer was a dolt and he treated you badly and somehow you began to believe you deserved to be treated that way. The truth is, may God forgive me, he deserved everything he ended up with."

Sam didn't hear anything further, just a low murmur and risked a tiny peak. Opening only one eye a mere slit he saw Tracy hugging Sali and patting her back. Snapping his eye shut again he struggled against the confusion he felt. What had Spencer ended up with? Wasn't he dead?

Sali was too keyed up to return to Sam and Samuel so she took off at a fast walk toward a small natural area of the park. There in the shade of fifty-year-old tamarisk trees she sank to the ground. Grasping a handful of the dry needles that had formed an inches thick cushion under her, she breathed deep of the distinctive scent, vaguely aware that it reminded her of the smell of rain. *Oh, if only Sam thought of me in the way Tracy thinks he does*, Sali whispered to herself. But, how could he? His ego must be shattered to be only half a man.

Leaning her head back against the papery, rough bark of a tree, Sali closed her eyes and tried to blank her mind of everything.

Almost against his will Sam felt drawn to her, as though he had to reassure himself of who and what she was. Unfortunately that would be easier said than done since he was still so confused. Especially with Tracy's observation ringing in his ears.

A quick word to Tracy assured him that Samuel would be looked after should he waken. Sam purposefully followed Sali's path to the far end of the park where the feathery leaves of Mediterranean Tamarisk trees, made a shady bower.

Sali made a perfect picture of angst, the column of her throat arched back to where her head rested on the tree trunk. Her knees were drawn up to her chest and her hands rested open, palms up on the ground. She almost seemed to be in an attitude of prayer or meditation and Sam hesitated disturbing her. What had seemed like a good idea laying on the quilt back in the picnic area now seemed the height of arrogance.

Sali's eyes slowly opened and she saw Sam standing a couple of yards away looking at her. "Are the kids alright?" she asked even as she rose to her feet in alarm.

"The kids are fine," Sam said quietly. Feeling suddenly awkward he shifted his feet. "Actually, I just wanted a little time alone with you"

Sam leaned against the rough, papery bark of the tree and looked at the grass. Letting the toes of his running shoes poke about, he strained at the sight as though the future was held there in the grass and soft, crumbly earth.

"This is a great picnic. Thanks for asking me," he began.

Simultaneously Sali said, "Too bad we didn't win the sack race."

Glancing quickly at each other they sank back into an uneasy silence. Sali could hear Tracy's words ringing in her brain. Was there some sort of body language they were emitting that made everyone think there was more to their relationship than there was? Or did everyone suffer from an incurably romantic and dirty mind?

Sam pulled a twig off the tree and brushed the long, feathery needles across the sun kissed skin of her upper arm, where it wrapped around her upper body in a parody of a hug. "Are you having a good time?"

"Sure. Everything is fine."

The twig raised higher, over her upper arm to her shoulder. Catching in the loose fabric of her cotton T-shirt Sam pulled on the stick to free the needles. "Did you lose a lot of weight recently or do you choose your clothes this loose on purpose?" As soon as Sam heard the words come out his mouth he knew he had made a mistake. Dropping the twig to the ground he dusted off his hands and searched his mind for some change of subject.

Sali laughed. "Actually, I do choose to wear loose clothes. They're more comfortable and I guess they fit my idea of who and what I am."

"And what would that be?" Sam asked, surprised that she hadn't walked away in anger from his rude remark.

"Oh, I'm a mother and I was a wife. I guess it's a uniform. I don't think about clothes anymore, or at least not like my friend Margot does. She uses clothes like costumes." Sali paused. "Actually, I could ask you the same question. You wear pretty baggy clothes." Realizing she was treading on thin ground, that his reasons may have to do with hiding his damaged body, she held her breath waiting for his reply.

Sam was surprised. He didn't think of his clothes as baggy and he didn't think of himself as someone whose clothes would be noticed.

Before he had a chance to formulate a response, Bridget leaped out from behind the tree with a shriek. Another child was close behind and Bridget took refuge behind Sam, using his body as a shield. The other kid, a skinny boy with so many freckles they ran together, and two missing front teeth, didn't seem to even attempt to swerve. He kept running in the same direction and slammed into Sam's mid-section. The impact knocked his breath from his body and doubled him over.

"Oh, my God, Sam are you okay?" Sali bent over to see Sam's face. Bridget and the other child took off running in another direction while Sam struggled to regain his breath. "Should I get help?" Sali was starting to feel panic. What if some injured part had been collided with, with enough impact to cause more damage?

Sam waved his hand at her to indicate he was alright but Sali wasn't convinced and started trying to force him to the ground.

"Sit dammit. I'll go get help!"

"Sali, I'm okay," Sam gasped.

"Where did he hit you? No, you don't have to tell me. That's okay. Forget I asked."

"In my gut, and I'm fine. It just knocked the wind out of my sails for a minute."

"Are you sure you didn't get hit in your... um... injury?" Sali's eyes made a betraying darting glance downward.

"I'm fine. Really." Sam shook his head. What was it with her? One minute she was telling him she wore baggy clothes as a uniform because she was a mother and a wife and the next she can't keep her eyes off his crotch.

One glance at her face told him that everything was far from fine and they walked wordlessly back to the colorful quilt rumpled in the shade where Samuel slept in sweaty oblivion.

Chapter Seven

Sali lay in bed watching the square of the window lighten as morning grew near. A dream hovered on the edge of consciousness; she and Sam had been kissing and touching and oh, so sweetly loving one another in almost the most physical way two people could. Just when their dream love had been about to be consummated she woke up feeling unsatisfied and needy. She considered again her decision to live without sex, and wondered if it was possible.

Naturally, her mind wandered to the extent of Sam's injuries and she tried to imagine what sort of blast could have ripped him apart and destroyed his chances of having a family. Was anything left or did it all just not work? At the same time that a feeling of pity for him washed over her, another came full of pity for herself since she would miss out, too if her plan was successful. Though, she told herself, a man like Sam Thompson would never have looked twice at her if he were a whole man. He'd marry a beautiful woman and have a houseful of his own babies, never considering Sali, who, at thirty-two was by no means ugly, but realistically considered herself merely acceptable.

Sam rolled over in bed and groaned though he knew

Sali felt a pang of guilt over not calling except when she was in dire straits. The last time was when Joe and Miranda had died. "No! Nothing like that," Sali rushed to assure her. "Actually, I'm having, uh, man trouble."

"A man! Holy cow and hallelujah!" Margot chortled across the phone lines. "How in the world did you meet a man? Ah, who cares! I'm just so glad you have." Margo settled back in the roomy office chair parked in front of the computer and propped her feet on the desk. Running a hand of red-tipped nails through her spikey red hair she gushed breathlessly, in a cheap parody of girlish confidence, "Tell me everything!"

"Well," Sali struggled for words. "He's my neighbor and he loves my kids and is so kind and thoughtful."

"Oh can the altruistic crap. What does he look like?"

Sali smiled, imagining Margo sweltering in her apartment in Las Vegas yet still finding the energy to get excited over girl-talk just like when they were teenagers. "He's tall, about six foot. Black hair, brown eyes, thin, glasses."

"Sounds like a damn accountant!" Though Margo loved Sali dearly, she often doubted her ability to see things rationally.

"No, no. He looks more like a composer. He has long, muscular legs and nice hands. Yes, he has nice hands." Sali felt her body heating up just thinking about Sam's hands. Gripping the phone tighter she fanned her face with the paperback novel she still held.

"So, what's the trouble? He loves your kids. He's nice. He's good looking. Does he have a job? Does he drink? Is he a bar fly?"

"He doesn't drink except for an occasional beer and I don't think he ever goes to bars. He doesn't have a job and that's the trouble. Or where it starts, anyway."

"Oh, he's thinking you'll support him with your mass

his injured muscles were getting better. His discomfort was of a more immediate nature. He had been having a dream about his neighbor and his body still betrayed the subject matter of that dream. For a few moments he allowed himself the luxury of imagining burying himself inside of Sali's lush, sweet body until the physical evidence of his thoughts became almost painful. Rising slowly, he stretched, and laughed to himself that if she were to check out his crotch this morning she'd be in for quite a surprise. His loose silk boxers tented out from the juncture of his legs, showing just how much he wished he really could live out his fantasy with Sali.

First letting icy needles of water hit him and shock him back to a semblance of normalcy, he slowly warmed up the spray of the state of the art showerhead he had installed. While soaping his body he idly considered the scars he still retained from the explosion. Since the damage had been mainly internal, ripped ligaments and tendons from the blast that had sent him cart wheeling across the machine room floor, there were few visible scars. The exception was one thin one that had been the result of a razor sharp piece of aluminum flying through the air after he had already been knocked to the ground. But that scar was something you would have to look for, not something immediately seen. The trouble was that because of it the scars on his psyche had been much more brutal.

As effective as a surgeon's knife the aluminum had sliced into his body and performed a near perfect vasectomy. What the injury didn't accomplish, scar tissue did and now his chances of impregnating a woman were practically nil. Thank goodness it hadn't affected the performance of his reproductive organs, though. They obviously had no problems, he told himself with a wry grin, considering his excessively excited state this morning.

Sam nodded. He knew the kids talked about his comings and goings and so he wasn't surprised that she knew he walked each morning. "I could look at your car. I know a little about mechanics."

Sliding back under the greasy old car, with his knuckles scraped raw and his back filled with the impression of road grit, Sam wished he'd just offered to hire a mechanic to do the job. In fact, he berated himself, instead of offering the use of a garden cart he should have had the car fixed for her weeks ago when it first broke down. The starter had gone out and though it wasn't a serious problem, he was having a hard time getting the gummy bolts out so that he could slide a shiny new one in place.

"Damn!" he grated when the bolt finally came free sending his knuckles into a sudden collision with the motor.

"How about a break for a beer?" Peering under the car Sali saw Sam sucking on his knuckles leaving a black smear on his lips.

Straightening with a groan, Sam leaned his hips on the front bumper and took a long, deep gulp off the cold beer. "Yuck," he grimaced and wiped a forearm experimentally across his greasy lips.

Sali reached up and rubbed her finger on the remaining spot until it was gone. Feeling his eyes on her she suddenly knew what a deer felt like caught in a car's headlights. She couldn't tear her eyes away as Sam stared back though she somehow managed to remove her finger.

"Mama!" Rocketing towards them was Bridget and up until her body actually collided with Sali's midriff their eyes stayed on one another.

Sali went back inside the house to find out what the commotion was that had got Bridget worked up while Sam quickly installed the new starter motor and testing it, found that it worked fine. Knocking briefly at the back door he

stepped inside and went right to the kitchen sink to wa his hands. "All fixed."

"Thank you so much, Sam. To think, the part cc only forty dollars and the garage would have charged me couple hundred." On impulse she raised onto her toes a kissed him softly on his cheek. Bridget, watching from t doorway, shrieked as loudly as she could until all the ki had assembled.

"Mama kissed Mr. Tom Son!"

Sam quickly leaned over and smacked a loud kiss Bridget's cheek proclaiming, "And now I've kissed you! Pa it on!" The impulsive gesture diffused what was a pote tially embarrassing situation as Bridget chased a relucta Will, smacking her own lips in aggressive intent. S mouthed a grateful "thanks" as she dished up bowls fragrant, mild chili to join the quesadillas already on t table.

Sali threw down the book she had been reading in fru tration. She'd spent an hour trying to make sense of t same paragraph. Usually an hour spent with a novel aft the kids were asleep helped wind her down but on th night she was unable to stop some inner spring that w wound too tight.

Confusing thoughts chattered around in her brain. SI knew that Sam would make a fine father for her childre and even an attentive and kind husband. But how was sI to attract a man who had no interest in sex? Margo, h friend from high school, would know and before the thoug! was even fully formed Sali was picking up the phone ar dialing.

"I know you must have a problem if you're wasting you measly income on a long distance phone call," Margo sa matter of factly as soon as the usual greetings were e changed. "Please don't tell me someone else has died!"

his injured muscles were getting better. His discomfort was of a more immediate nature. He had been having a dream about his neighbor and his body still betrayed the subject matter of that dream. For a few moments he allowed himself the luxury of imagining burying himself inside of Sali's lush, sweet body until the physical evidence of his thoughts became almost painful. Rising slowly, he stretched, and laughed to himself that if she were to check out his crotch this morning she'd be in for quite a surprise. His loose silk boxers tented out from the juncture of his legs, showing just how much he wished he really could live out his fantasy with Sali.

First letting icy needles of water hit him and shock him back to a semblance of normalcy, he slowly warmed up the spray of the state of the art showerhead he had installed. While soaping his body he idly considered the scars he still retained from the explosion. Since the damage had been mainly internal, ripped ligaments and tendons from the blast that had sent him cart wheeling across the machine room floor, there were few visible scars. The exception was one thin one that had been the result of a razor sharp piece of aluminum flying through the air after he had already been knocked to the ground. But that scar was something you would have to look for, not something immediately seen. The trouble was that because of it the scars on his psyche had been much more brutal.

As effective as a surgeon's knife the aluminum had sliced into his body and performed a near perfect vasectomy. What the injury didn't accomplish, scar tissue did and now his chances of impregnating a woman were practically nil. Thank goodness it hadn't affected the performance of his reproductive organs, though. They obviously had no problems, he told himself with a wry grin, considering his excessively excited state this morning.

Sam set off for his morning walk, briskly taking one of his favorite routes that took him past some larger homes on larger lots on The Hill. Here the houses were set well back from the street, surrounded by huge trees like Sali's backyard elm, and because of the winding paths following the contours of the hills, traffic was few and slow.

One house in particular always intrigued him: a deep covered porch stretched across the front and a tiny balcony above gave a friendly open look to the place. The cream siding and dark green trim was offset by lighter green trim on curlicues of wooden adornment.

A red and blue sign indicated that it was for sale and being handled by the same realtor who had handled the purchase for Sam's house. This was a large place, though, and he had no justification for owning such a roomy home. He would just be lonely, rattling around there by himself. Besides, Sali's hooligans had grown on him and he couldn't imagine not living next door to them, drinking lemonade with Albert or hanging Bridget's pictures on the fridge.

He envisioned, briefly, a tree house built by Albert in one particularly suited elm. Sam considered that Albert would have great fun with the garbage in this neighborhood. Bridget could hold forth on that stage of a front porch and Sali would be able to grow all the leggy, weedy garden patches her heart desired on the large lot. Will and Jo could run and frolic in knee deep meadow grass while Stephanie could surely find a place to curl up with a book in the shade somewhere out of the way of all the noise and shenanigans. The front walk was a little bumpy but it wouldn't be long before Samuel's halting baby steps would progress to the point where a popcorn push toy could be rolled at great speed along the lumpy concrete. And at the end of the day, he could climb the long flight of stairs to that balconied bedroom above the porch and in the cool breeze from the open door he could hold Sali in his arms.

Shaking his head he banished the dream and turned resolutely away from the large house where he might have raised a family had things been different. Nodding at an older couple walking a shaggy terrier Sam clenched his fisted hands in the roomy pockets of his shorts and briskly walked away.

The diner was full of the usual crowd as Sam sidled up to his stool. The same two factory workers sat next to him but on this morning they were quiet, sipping their coffee in between huge bites of ham, egg and hash browns dripping yolk and grease.

The biggest, fattest one, aged-grayed T-shirt straining across his belly, saw Sam staring and he scowled to show his displeasure in being watched. Just then a familiar shrill voice called out, "Why hello! I didn't expect to see you here!" Mrs. Browning was bustling across the diner, dodging tables and chairs full of interested faces.

Sam swallowed a scalding sip of coffee and forced a smile of greeting on his face. The big guy next to him did the same, calling out in a resigned voice, "Hi Bertha," but Bertha Browning kept on coming and with barely a nod of recognition at her son-in-law she zeroed in on Sam.

"It was such a pleasure to see you again at church with dear Sali."

The men nearby looked on with undisguised interest. Fiddling with the coffee mug, Sam merely nodded to acknowledge her words.

"Well, I said to my daughter; she's married to Hank here;" a nod in the fatter guy's direction identified him, "that Sali could do worse than Sam Thompson. I remember hearing about your accident over in Circleville at the plant. What a shame. But look at you now! You're fit as a fiddle. Got a large settlement as I recall."

Flabbergasted was too tame a word for what Sam felt. Not only had her loud, snoopy comments drawn the attention of her son-in-law and friend, half the diner's other occupants were watching with avid interest, too.

"Thanks for your interest, Mrs. Browning but as you yourself said, I'm fit as a fiddle now."

"But didn't you have some long-term disability to get such a large settlement?" This, then was the heart of the matter and Sam saw her eyes grow beady as she swooped in for the kill.

"Yes." Sam kept a little half smile on his face with difficulty. The entire diner was silent, waiting for him to elaborate on the extent of his injuries but he merely took another sip from his coffee and stared pleasantly back at the nosy woman's face.

Hank, never known for his tact, realized that this was the man he had heard gossip about. Thrusting his big, beefy hand out toward Sam he introduced himself gruffly, "Reese, Hank Reese." After shaking hands he squinted one eye, looked Sam up and down, and commented, "I knew Sali's husband, Spencer. Worked with him. Good man. Left a bunch of kids."

Sam knew that this was the shorthand of men; that abbreviated language that only another man can understand, and his years at the factory made it all completely clear to him. "Yes, a bunch of good kids." Translated it meant that he liked those kids, recognized their worth and wasn't going to try to replace Spencer. Hank nodded in appreciation.

Mrs. Browning, however, was far from being as astute as her son-in-law. "So..." she started coyly, batting her eyelashes in the most revolting manner. Sam stared in disgusted fascination as her too red lips formed the words, "...are there wedding bells on the horizon?"

Sam gave a quick snort of a laugh, which could be taken to mean several different things, but confirmed nothing and after a few more idle comments he made his excuses and left the diner.

He had to deliberately slow his walk as he neared home or else he'd have to take another circuit around the block just to cool down. He considered how Bertha Browning just seemed to set him off and decided to put her out of his mind as deliberately as he had turned his walk from the usual loping stride to a more sedate stroll as his house came into view.

Sali held the lacey curtains to the side and anxiously watched for the mailman. She expected the Social Security checks today and with luck she would be able to get the car fixed. Although it was possible to get around without one, having motorized wheels made shopping and errands so much easier. As the end of summer loomed and Fall school clothes shopping became a necessity, the car would absolutely be required.

As she stood at the front window scanning the sidewalk for signs of John the mailman, she noticed Sam striding down the street. His limp, what little of it she had ever seen, was almost completely gone now. He looked a little harried but when he glanced up and saw her standing at the window his face clcarcd to a pleasant look of greeting. At his gesture she opened the door and stepped out into the bright, hot sunshine.

"You look like you're in a good mood," Sali commented.

Sam was silent, looking back at Sali's lush body, youthful clothes, wild hair and slightly anxious expression.

"I'm waiting for the mailman. It's payday and I need to get my car fixed" Sali wondered what it was about her neighbor that turned her mind to mush and make her say the most idiotic things. "Have you been for your walk?"

Sam nodded. He knew the kids talked about his comings and goings and so he wasn't surprised that she knew he walked each morning. "I could look at your car. I know a little about mechanics."

Sliding back under the greasy old car, with his knuckles scraped raw and his back filled with the impression of road grit, Sam wished he'd just offered to hire a mechanic to do the job. In fact, he berated himself, instead of offering the use of a garden cart he should have had the car fixed for her weeks ago when it first broke down. The starter had gone out and though it wasn't a serious problem, he was having a hard time getting the gummy bolts out so that he could slide a shiny new one in place.

"Damn!" he grated when the bolt finally came free sending his knuckles into a sudden collision with the motor.

"How about a break for a beer?" Peering under the car Sali saw Sam sucking on his knuckles leaving a black smear on his lips.

Straightening with a groan, Sam leaned his hips on the front bumper and took a long, deep gulp off the cold beer. "Yuck," he grimaced and wiped a forearm experimentally across his greasy lips.

Sali reached up and rubbed her finger on the remaining spot until it was gone. Feeling his eyes on her she suddenly knew what a deer felt like caught in a car's headlights. She couldn't tear her eyes away as Sam stared back though she somehow managed to remove her finger.

"Mama!" Rocketing towards them was Bridget and up until her body actually collided with Sali's midriff their eyes stayed on one another.

Sali went back inside the house to find out what the commotion was that had got Bridget worked up while Sam quickly installed the new starter motor and testing it, found that it worked fine. Knocking briefly at the back door he stepped inside and went right to the kitchen sink to wash his hands. "All fixed."

"Thank you so much, Sam. To think, the part cost only forty dollars and the garage would have charged me a couple hundred." On impulse she raised onto her toes and kissed him softly on his cheek. Bridget, watching from the doorway, shrieked as loudly as she could until all the kids had assembled.

"Mama kissed Mr. Tom Son!"

Sam quickly leaned over and smacked a loud kiss on Bridget's cheek proclaiming, "And now I've kissed you! Pass it on!" The impulsive gesture diffused what was a potentially embarrassing situation as Bridget chased a reluctant Will, smacking her own lips in aggressive intent. Sali mouthed a grateful "thanks" as she dished up bowls of fragrant, mild chili to join the quesadillas already on the table.

Sali threw down the book she had been reading in frustration. She'd spent an hour trying to make sense of the same paragraph. Usually an hour spent with a novel after the kids were asleep helped wind her down but on this night she was unable to stop some inner spring that was wound too tight.

Confusing thoughts chattered around in her brain. She knew that Sam would make a fine father for her children, and even an attentive and kind husband. But how was she to attract a man who had no interest in sex? Margo, her friend from high school, would know and before the thought was even fully formed Sali was picking up the phone and dialing.

"I know you must have a problem if you're wasting your measly income on a long distance phone call," Margo said matter of factly as soon as the usual greetings were exchanged. "Please don't tell me someone else has died!"

Sali felt a pang of guilt over not calling except when she was in dire straits. The last time was when Joe and Miranda had died. "No! Nothing like that," Sali rushed to assure her. "Actually, I'm having, uh, man trouble."

"A man! Holy cow and hallelujah!" Margot chortled across the phone lines. "How in the world did you meet a man? Ah, who cares! I'm just so glad you have." Margo settled back in the roomy office chair parked in front of the computer and propped her feet on the desk. Running a hand of red-tipped nails through her spikey red hair she gushed breathlessly, in a cheap parody of girlish confidence, "Tell me everything!"

"Well," Sali struggled for words. "He's my neighbor and he loves my kids and is so kind and thoughtful."

"Oh can the altruistic crap. What does he look like?"

Sali smiled, imagining Margo sweltering in her apartment in Las Vegas yet still finding the energy to get excited over girl-talk just like when they were teenagers. "He's tall, about six foot. Black hair, brown eyes, thin, glasses."

"Sounds like a damn accountant!" Though Margo loved Sali dearly, she often doubted her ability to see things rationally.

"No, no. He looks more like a composer. He has long, muscular legs and nice hands. Yes, he has nice hands." Sali felt her body heating up just thinking about Sam's hands. Gripping the phone tighter she fanned her face with the paperback novel she still held.

"So, what's the trouble? He loves your kids. He's nice. He's good looking. Does he have a job? Does he drink? Is he a bar fly?"

"He doesn't drink except for an occasional beer and I don't think he ever goes to bars. He doesn't have a job and that's the trouble. Or where it starts, anyway."

"Oh, he's thinking you'll support him with your mass

wealth." Margo's words dripped with sarcasm.

Sali laughed at the image that evoked. "No, actually he had a job but was injured and got some kind of settlement so he doesn't work. At least he doesn't go to a job. Truthfully, I don't know what he does. But it's the injury I have a problem with."

"Um, he has legs cause you said they were long and muscular. He has arms because you have to have arms to have hands at the ends. Is he all scarred up?" Margo sat up straight in her chair letting her feet fall to the floor. Stretching above the desk she adjusted the air conditioner to blow more directly on her, feeling it riffle through her hair.

"Actually, I haven't seen any scars. The problem is that he told the kids that there was an explosion at his work and it hurt him so that he couldn't have children. Margot, I'm afraid he lost his, uh, his..."

"Oh, my God. It got blown off? Holy cow. That's dreadful! How do you two do it?"

"Do what?"

"You know. How do you do the deed? Dance the horizontal tango? Get it on?"

Sali shuddered at the images Margo was dazzling her with. It all sounded so raw and primitive and somehow very interesting. "That's the problem, actually. You see, we haven't done anything. I don't think he can. And what is worrying me is that I know I could be very happy with him and I can learn to live without sex..."

"Live without sex?" Margot shouted.

"Well," Sali whispered violently, "what do you propose? If he can't do it he can't do it. That's not the problem."

Margot held her head in her hands with the phone cradled between her ear and her shoulder. "Haven't I taught you anything? God, first you take up with that cheating, drinking, sleaze bag Spencer and now you go to the opposite extreme and get hooked up with an eunuch."

"Margo, listen to me. Ignore all that." Sali waved her hand in the air as though Margo could see the impatient gesture. "It's my life. What I need you to tell me is how I can attract a man that isn't attracted to sex. Food doesn't seem to be important to him so inviting him to dinner won't impress him. He doesn't go out at night. I don't know what to do."

"Okay, let me think. He likes the kids? Keep him involved with them. Does he do things for you?" Against her better judgment Margot was in her element now, giving advice and using her keen mind to figure out all the angles and new approaches.

"Yes, in fact, today he fixed my car for me. And he buys stuff for us. I told you he was nice."

"Hmmm. Men like to be needed. If he can't be a man in bed maybe you have to let him be a man everywhere else. Encourage him to hang out, go places with you, fix things that are broken, mow the damn grass. But, you'd better still flirt with him. Even if he can't do it he'll still want to know that you find him attractive and wish he could do it. But you can't act like you miss it too much or else he'll feel like less of a man. Oh, God. I don't know. Have you seen it?"

"Seen what?" Sali was still stuck on imagining showing Sam she wished he could "do it."

"The injuries." Margot shuddered.

"No! We've only ever kissed but it was pretty good."

"Oh, Sali, I hope you know what you're doing. No sex? I guess he might be good practice for you as long as you don't do anything rash and marry him. That's a life sentence, you know."

After catching up with their lives, Sali's kids and Margot's job as a 21 dealer in a Las Vegas casino, they said good bye with promises to talk more often without waiting for a catastrophe.

Sali placed the phone on its cradle and contemplated how to go about encouraging Sam as Margot had suggested. Those things came easily for Margot. Always a little wild, a little loud and a little bold, Margot had grown into an intimidating woman. But she knew how to make a man want to please her.

Years before on a rare night out, Sali had observed Margot, seemingly oblivious to the riff raff in the corner bar where Spencer had talked the two women into accompanying him, get more attention than Sali would ever want. One minute Margot had been animatedly telling Sali about a casino in Vegas and the next several men were vying for her attention. Sali felt she had become invisible in the glow of Margot's personality.

The next day Sali waited until Sam went out onto his back porch. He was carrying a coffee mug and sheath of papers that looked like reports. As soon as he had settled at the tiny table there Sali sauntered over to the picket fence dividing the properties.

Sam looked up and saw her standing there, looking uncertain and unbelievably young with Samuel balanced on her hip. "What's up?"

"Oh, I was just wondering if you havc a spare cup of coffee. I'm all out and it sure sounds good."

"I just brewed a pot. Come on over."

Sali walked around to the front gate and then to the back yard trying to remember all the clever things she'd rehearsed earlier. Helping herself to a cup of coffee she joined Sam at the table. After a few moments of trying to keep Samuel on her lap she gave up and set him in the grass. "What are those papers? They look serious?" Leaning towards Sam she let her hair barely brush his arm as she tilted her face to see the top page.

"Investment reports. That's how I keep busy when I'm not replacing starter motors or taping pictures on my refrigerator." Something wasn't right here. Sali was acting strangely though he wasn't sure exactly in what way.

"Oh." Sali's mind went blank again.

"It's how I make my living now. I used the settlement from the accident and invested the lion's share."

"Oh." She scrambled for something to say. "How interesting." She cringed as realization dawned that her voice sounded vague and confused even to herself.

Sam threw back his head and laughed. "Actually, it is interesting. To me. Because every time a number changes it means my money has changed. The fun part is guessing what will happen next, anticipating it and changing my investment accordingly."

"Don't you have to go through an office or a broker or something?"

As he saw real interest blossom on her face he warmed to his subject. After explaining that he did all of his trading on the Internet, they went inside to the bedroom he had converted to an office and he showed her his computer, logging on so she could see how he kept track of his portfolio. Soon Samuel grew restless and started patting Sali's cheek, an indication that he wanted her undivided interest. Sali glanced at her watch and saw that the Disney movie the kids were watching would be just about over and lunchtime was rapidly approaching.

"How about lunch with us? I made a killer potato salad earlier."

Sam hesitated at the reminder that she had been accused of murder by the men in the diner and saw Sali's face fall. "I'd love to. What shall I bring?" and was amazed to see the intense pleasure that streaked across her features at his acceptance.

The kids gleefully set the table and at the last minute Bridget ran outside and picked some of the dying marigolds. Sali unobtrusively rinsed them off before arranging them in a water glass on the table. Sam raised his eyebrows in question and she mouthed back "ants" at which he nodded in understanding.

After lunch Sali washed dishes while Sam played Go Fish with the kids at the table. When Jo lost for the fifth time in a row she dropped her head onto the table top and began to cry. "Aw, it's not that bad, Jo," Sam crooned as he picked her up and held her in his lap. "Let me tell you a story..." and so began the most foolish tall tale Sali had ever heard. The kids were all fascinated and asked endless questions and in the end begged for more but Sam explained that he had work to do and would see them later.

Pausing briefly at Sali's side where she stood at the sink he glanced at her mouth and wished he had the courage to kiss her again but with the avid audience sitting round the table he felt a little intimidated.

Sali looked back at Sam's face and saw the direction his eyes took. When realization dawned that Sam actually was wanting to kiss her, she grew flustered and felt her hand flutter at her hair, tucking a loose curl behind her ear.

Sam watched color blossom in Sali's cheeks, and was unable to restrain his grin when she started fiddling with her hair leaving a trail of dish soap bubbles dangling from her ear like some demented earring. "Thanks for lunch. I'll see you later," he said softly and briefly touched her shoulder as he turned to leave.

As soon as the back door shut Bridget dragged Sali's attention away from whatever far place it was hiding by screeching, "You got bubbles on your ear!" Sali groaned and angrily swiped at the white froth with the dishtowel.

Sitting in front of the computer later, Sam had a hard time paying attention to the numbers and symbols on the screen. He wasn't absolutely certain but he thought Sali had been flirting with him. For one thing, in plain sight on the counter was a brand new can of coffee, which made her excuse to have coffee with him earlier an out and out lie. The trouble was, the only reason he could come up with for her to lie was that she was looking for an excuse to see him. The absurdity of the thought made him smile. Her kids had no trouble finding excuses to come knocking on his door.

Completely abandoning his attempt at researching some new stock that had recently gone public, Sam leaned back in his chair and put his hands behind his head. Tilting his head back he stared at the corner of the room as though a re-play of lunch was displayed there.

Sali had seemed to find several excuses to hand things to Sam directly, letting her hands touch his softly each time, lingering just a tiny bit longer than absolutely necessary. He had caught her looking at him while he was listening to one of the kids and she had looked away quickly when he returned the gaze. And then there was that ridiculous moment when she fiddled with her hair and left soap bubbles hanging off her ear. Just thinking about it set Sam off laughing and the idea that he was sitting alone in his house laughing out loud made him laugh all the harder.

Sali was carrying a bag of garbage out to the dented metal can behind the shed when she heard laughing coming from Sam's house. Her head jerked in that direction and she stopped to listen. She couldn't hear any other voice; maybe he was on the phone.

She had never before heard him laugh quite so loudly or without inhibition before and it took a moment for her to recognize that she was jealous of whoever it was who could give him such pleasure that he could laugh like that. Maybe he and whomever he was laughing with were laughing at her and her ridiculous attempts at flirting. Feeling her cheeks get hot with mortification she nearly ran back into the house hoping to hide not only from Sam, but also from her wayward thoughts.

No matter what Tracy had said when they were at the picnic, Sali couldn't convince herself that she was anything other than a drudge. Serving up barely edible slop to a bunch of fatherless, unruly children, trudging about in her unattractively baggy clothes, and uneducated about such things as the Internet when the whole rest of the world knew exactly what it was about. Feeling suddenly boring and dull she deposited the bag in the can and returned to the house dispirited and quiet.

Chapter Eight

She was having the dream again. Even though some part of Sali's mind was aware that this was a dream, another part of her urged her to just give in to these brief moments of pleasure. She moved restlessly in her bed and allowed the dream to suck her in to a sensuous fantasyland.

Sam and she were dancing. Slowly their bodies moved together as one, his strong hands gently caressing her back in small circles of heat, her breasts flattened against his hard chest.

Burying her face into his shoulder she drew in a deep breath that seemed to carry the very essence of him. Feeling his breath at her cheek she turned her head slightly and felt his lips brush her temple. Keeping her eyes tightly closed she lifted her chin ever so slightly, just enough, and then his mouth was on hers.

If the Fourth of July kiss was a sparkler this one was a cherry bomb. It exploded in her belly like liquid fire, spreading out to her limbs leaving her weak and shaky. Clutching Sam's wide shoulders she clung to him shamelessly, ever seeking a deeper fulfillment, hearts beating a wild tattoo in unison as they mimicked a greater intimacy with their tongues.

Sam's hands dropped lower, to the curve of Sali's back. Then slowly higher again and around to her sides. She willed them higher. She wordlessly begged them to sweep around to her aching breasts. Keeping her lower body and mouth against Sam's hard, pulsing frame she pulled her chest away, giving him access to the soft parts of her crying out for his touch. Closer his hands came and she moaned in need.

Brushing the sides of her swollen breasts, Sam's hands tortured her senses. It was as though her mind had moved south, and lodged there since every bit of her sensibilities were there.

Closer, teasing, cruel need ate at her and her kisses became ravenous, trying in some wordless way to convey to him what she craved. Finally, his hands found her and held the soft mounds in his sturdy hands, nimble fingers wreaking havoc with nerve endings already overly sensitized.

Sam rolled over in bed, idly thinking of his dream from the other night. The sheet felt rough to his overheated skin and threw it back in frustration. How many years had it been since he felt the need to entertain such fantasies? With a groan he gave in and imagined kissing Sali. As his subconscious took over he drifted into an uneasy, dream-filled sleep.

Her skin was so soft beneath his lips he marveled that his heat wasn't burning her. He felt the small movement she made, lifting her face to him, offering herself, giving in. Lips meeting he nudged hers open and found her tongue.

Trembling with the effort to control himself, go slowly, test her desires at every turn, Sam let his mouth tell her how much he wanted her while his hands itched to control her flesh and make it scream his name.

Finally, his hands found her and held the soft mounds of her full breasts in his sturdy hands, nimble fingers teasing the peaks. A whimper of pleasure and then the need built again, finding other places and other needs to satisfy. And Sam found them, slowly tempting her flesh into a raging fire of hunger, threatening to consume her in its wake.

Pulling her closer, Sam ran his hands down her back to the very curve of her buttocks. He felt her shudder and press her lush curves closer. The feel of her flattened breasts pressed against him drove him mad and his hands, of their own volition, crept higher. Sali pulled away slightly and at first his heart stopped thinking she was rejecting him but instead he discovered she was encouraging him. Unbelievably she was encouraging his explorations.

As in all dreams, some of the pieces didn't fit quite right and Sali found that she and Sam were now on their sides, on a bed of softest silk, their bodies pressed together from toes to temple with nothing in between. Her hands were sweeping, seeking to give him pleasure and her reward was a deep moan from his chest.

Sam marveled as her small, cool hand swept down his heated flesh, along his hip. Her other hand was at his cheek, holding his head in place for her mouth to keep contact. Gasping for breath he pulled away from her greedy grasp and kissed her along her smooth jaw line, working his way down.

Sali's hands both held his head, curling her fingers through his hair as he worked magic on her heated flesh.

Sali felt a keening sound of desire raging in her throat. Giving freedom to it, she gasped and groaned her need for his touch. Her hand crept bravely, slowly down his hip to the place where the bone jutted out and then over. Seeking him, searching for some proof of his desire her smooth palm made a feathery sweep of his lower abdomen. Smooth skin met her questing fingers. Again her hand swept across his flesh and again she found nothing.

Sam felt himself being dragged down into a place of sensation. Soft, warm and wet, he sunk into pure desire. Feeling her small, cool hand sweeping across his lower abdomen he mindlessly begged for her to want him more, need him more, find him and in the finding, help him find his own satisfaction. But suddenly her hands traveled up his body, over his belly, chest and neck. Over his night roughened cheeks to his hair. Catching in the strands there, her fingers curled and held and then pushed. Down, down he sank, into an oblivion that could be passion or could be death. He accepted the blackness of the depth of this confusion under her hands that held him in thrall.

Confusion stumbled across her dazed brain as she felt for him, desperate to find the evidence of his desire. Again nothing and she slowed her search to find that he was as smooth as Barbie doll's boyfriend; no jutting manhood or sensitive skin met her fingers and the keening groan from her own throat became a screech of betrayal, of pain as she woke with a start.

Little Samuel's cries had reached a crescendo of terror. Sali wrenched her passion glazed eyes open and swung her feet over to the edge of the bed. A dream. Just a dream. Samuel was crying while she'd been having an erotic dream about her neighbor.

Sam was still dreaming but the scene had shifted. The very air felt thick, too thick to breathe and his stomach heaved. He was on the rolling deck of a boat and Will was calling out to him from somewhere in the misty water. He dove in to save the small boy and just as the water closed over his head he felt the strong hands move from his head to grasping his shoulder and dragging him back to the surface. "I have to find Will," he said weakly, struggling to get away.

"Sam! Sam! Wake up. There's a gas leak, we have to get you out of here. Please, Sam, wake up." Sali felt real panic as she shook his shoulders. Finally, deciding she could wait no longer she hooked a hand under each arm and started dragging him toward the door. Crashing into the side of a nightstand Sali nearly lost her momentum but got a new grasp and pulled again. From far off she could hear the sirens signifying help was on its way and was grateful that she could rely on Albert.

As the fresh air from the open front door washed over Sam he barely came to consciousness and seeing Sali's face above his, her thin cotton nightgown billowing in the breeze his befuddled mind struggled to make sense. "Let's go back to bed, Sali," he mumbled. He reached up with his hands to pull her down to him.

"Hold on, Sam. We're almost there."

Suddenly the smell of natural gas and the surrealistic images of his house in total darkness aligned with the utter nausea he was assailed with. Twisting to the side he managed to pull away from Sali's grasp. She was going to kill him, just as she had Spencer, he realized.

"Oh, no! You're not going to do me in!" But in his weakened state she was stronger and pulled him to the front door just as firemen reached them and quickly lifted him up and to the safety of the front yard and fresh air.

Sam didn't even have the energy to open his eyes so he tried to use his other senses to figure out where he was and what was going on. Sali's voice was quavering with emotion and a deeper male voice answered her back in calm tones.

"The baby woke me up. He's teething and cranky. I was rocking him in the open back door when I smelled the gas. I woke my son, Albert up to help me sniff out where it was coming from." A shaky breath bordering on a sob wracked her body. "I still couldn't figure it out but it was so strong and I was afraid. I woke up all the kids and sent them out to the front yard and then I went to Sam's to see if he could smell it."

"Who is Sam, Ma'am?"

"That's him, Sam Thompson" she quavered, pointing at the still form surrounded by paramedics, "The man I pulled out. As soon as I got to his yard I knew it was coming from inside and so I ran around to the back door and went in. Thank God he keeps it unlocked but if it hadn't been I was going to break the window to get in. I was yelling for him to wake up the whole time."

"And I was yelling, too," Will's small voice added.

"Yes, you were and doing a fine job of it, sweetie." Sali paused to hug her young son before continuing. "When I got inside I knew not to turn on any lights. The smell was so strong I was afraid even a tiny spark would ignite the gas."

"And where did you find him, Ma'am?"

"He was in bed. I couldn't wake him up. I tried and tried and shook him, but I couldn't wake him up." Suddenly the horror of that helplessness washed over her and she began to cry in earnest.

Sam feebly tried to lift a hand, to show her he was all right. "Sali," he whispered around the oxygen mask that was strapped to his face.

"Oh, Sam!" The soft weight of her breasts on his chest combined with her tears dropping on his cheek roused him enough to weakly pat her shoulder.

"I was so scared, Sam. I thought you were going to die."

"Ma'am, please…" a paramedic said as he gently extricated her from Sam's arms.

In moments he was sitting up, still feeling sick to his stomach but well enough to refuse to go to the hospital. After the paramedics had instructed him to write out his refusal and reasons on a form, they packed up and left, leaving the fire department behind to stand guard while the gas company isolated Sam's house from the main gas line. Warning Sam to not enter his house until the leak was located and repaired, and it was thoroughly aired out, the trucks all pulled away leaving him in Sali's care.

It took a few moments to settle the kids back down after the excitement but soon they were all in bed again. Sali led Sam to the sofa, and covered him with a light blanket. Placing a glass of water and a bucket next to the makeshift bed, just in case he got sick she realized that her hands were still shaking. Collapsing on the floor next to him she lay her head along the sofa cushions.

"I'm all right now, Sali. You can go to bed." He lay his hand on the crown of her head and felt the shudders quaking through her body. "Oh, don't cry, darlin', it's all over now."

She raised her head and gave him one long anguished look before he managed to get his arms around her in a heart-stopping hug. Rocking slowly they held on to each other and Sam realized that no matter what anyone else said, he knew Sali was not capable of killing anyone. She was gentle and brave and strong. He pulled her closer so that her head was cradled in his hands against his chest.

As Sali lay in the safety of Sam's arms, she realized that in this case, the safety he offered wasn't physical safety but emotional safety. Too tired and overwrought to explore what that meant, she felt her trembling subside and drifted off to sleep to the beat of Sam's heart against her cheek

It wasn't the sun streaming through lace curtains that woke him. And it wasn't the smell of burning toast or the languid weight of a woman's head on his shoulder or the tantalizing sensation of her arm draped across his side. It was a giggle. Such a small sound but it seemed to echo in his pounding head causing him to open his eyes and see a blurry crowd of children staring at him and Sali entwined in each other's arms on the sofa. Memory assailed him, explaining why his glasses were missing, why he was lay-ing on his neighbor's sofa in his boxer shorts, and why his head throbbed

"You're awake!" screamed Bridget. "Why are you and Mama sleeping on the sofa?" Though Sam could remem-ber how it came about that he and Sali fell asleep together he couldn't, for the life of him, explain why she would seek comfort in his arms nor why he would offer it so willingly.

Sali's eyes popped open with a start and she groaned when she saw the kids. "Great," she muttered as she extri-cated herself from Sam's arms. Swinging her legs to the floor she ran a hand through the tangled curls running riot on her head.

Looking around at the sea of expectant faces Sali no-ticed one whose avid curiosity pinned her with the inten-sity of its stare. The kids must have let Mrs. Browning in, and there she stood, not 4 feet away in obvious thrall of the scandal unfolding before her eyes.

"Hank heard about your trouble on the police scanner and called me right up this morning so I thought I'd pop over and see if there was anything I could do to help." A glistening pink tongue darted out to stroke her upper, red-dened lip and her eyes flickered over Sali in a gesture of dismissal before stopping to light on Sam.

Baby Samuel patted her knee from his precarious stance near the sofa and said the most apropos thing Sali had heard in a long time, "Wow."

Albert scowled darkly at his mother. "I made toast for the little kids." His eyes studiously avoided Sam's as he quickly turned and stomped from the room.

"Thanks, honey," Sali called out to his rapidly retreating back. "I guess I was just so tired I lay down here and fell asleep."

Realizing he was still wearing the silk boxers he had been wearing in bed last night, Sam wrapped the light blanket around himself and whispered in Sali's ear. Raising her eyebrows, she sent the kids scurrying to the kitchen. Going into her bedroom she returned moments later with her baggiest pair of elastic waist shorts and handed them over. Wordlessly Sam pulled them on under cover of the light blanket and then tried to stand.

Quickly Sali went to his side and supported him as he walked to the bathroom. As soon as she was sure he had made it inside okay she and Mrs. Browning followed the noise of the children to the kitchen where they had toast, jelly, peanut butter and a few cracked eggs smeared across the table.

"I guess this means that the rumors I've been hearing are true," the older lady said breathlessly.

"Oh, my," Sali whispered as she eyed the messes, both figurative and literal, around her. "And what rumors might those be?" Her voice was weary and a little rough from crying last night but she made fast work of the housekeeping disaster while the intrepid Bertha Browning watched silently. Moments later when Sam appeared leaning against the doorjamb the table was clean, coffee was perking and the kids were happily drinking orange juice. "How do you feel?"

"Hmmm, like a steam roller drove over my head. But that coffee smells like it might fix me up." He sat heavily in one of the chairs and put his head in his hands. "I guess I owe you my life."

"Hey, that could be interesting. You can be my slave now!" Sali felt giddy after the terror of the night and the new problem with the town's biggest gossip standing with stout legs firmly in place on the shiny linoleum floor.

"Just don't ask me to change Samuel's diaper. Anything but that!" He put his hands up in mock surrender. Will giggled wildly at the silly adult horseplay.

"I just don't know what the Pastor is going to say when he hears of this," Mrs. Browning clicked her tongue in gleeful disapproval.

Sparing a brief glance at her, Sam looked at the tow-headed young boy next to him and said seriously, "You know, Will, I heard you calling me last night. I didn't hear your Mama but I heard you." Catching Sali's eye he winked at her. Will ducked his head in embarrassment and pleasure.

"What kind of an example is this to these dear fatherless children?" Though she was obviously trying for a tone of censure, Hank's mother-in-law couldn't disguise her excitement at watching a scandal unfold before her very eyes. "Obviously you two will be getting married now that you've jumped the gun and..."

Sali cut her off with a harsh "hush!" coupled with her fierce Irish glare.

Sali poured Sam a cup of coffee with slightly shaky hands. Albert's face was serious as he watched the dark liquid splash into the heavy, white crockery cup when suddenly he blurted out, "You slept with my mom and now you have to marry her." Albert, with his black and white way of looking at the world could see no other solution.

"Al, it wasn't the kind of 'sleeping together' that means we have to get married. We were tired and we fell asleep."

Sam was out of his element, treading on thin ice. If the conversation got any stickier he would have to talk about sex and he wasn't sure Sali would like that at all.

"I know I told you we didn't need you but if you are going to be kissing and sleeping with my mom you have to marry her. It's just the right thing to do!"

Startled Sali jerked her gaze to her oldest child. They had had this talk before? Sam rubbed his fingers through his hair, unconsciously massaging his aching head. "Last night we had unusual circumstances. Your mother saved my life by dragging me out of the house and I'm sure that the panic exhausted her. She wore herself out and fell asleep and I was in no condition to wake her up or carry her to her room."

Albert was shaking his head. "Those are just excuses."

Mrs. Browning's head swiveled back and forth on her thin stalk of a neck as though this were just a tennis match she was watching at the local country club.

Sam nodded. "I understand where you're coming from. And they are excuses, but they're valid. The only reason to get married is because you're in love and want to spend the rest of your lives together. Your mother and I are not in love." As soon as the words left his mouth Sam realized that he wasn't sure they were true. He spared a glance for Sali and saw that she held a look of hurt resignation.

Deflated, Albert looked down at the now clean table top. "Yeah, I know."

Sam awkwardly put his arms around the tall thin boy and was surprised when he was hugged back fiercely in return. "Al, if I wanted to get married your mother would be the perfect wife and if I wanted to be a father I can't think of any children I would rather have than you and your brothers and sisters."

"Well, that settles it, then! I'll just tell the pastor that you two will be in to talk to him!" As fast as her support hose could carry her, the old biddy was out the back door and trotting around the side of the house toward her Lincoln Continental parked crookedly at the curb. Sali didn't even have time to complete her gasp of shock.

Feeling tears spring to her eyes she watched Albert and Sam hug. Spencer had never seemed to understand Albert. He wanted him to be tough and athletic. Instead he was mystified to find this serious, intellectual inventor as his son. In some ways, she realized, Sam and Albert were very much alike. The two, tall and thin, with heads bowed in some private communion, obviously understood each other.

Breaking the spell, Bridget's shrill voice gleefully proclaimed, "Hooray! Mama and Mr. Tom Son are gettin married!"

"No, we're not!" both Sam and Sali proclaimed, looking in startled embarrassment at each other. Just then the phone rang. Glad for the interruption Sali grabbed the receiver before it rang a second time.

"Hello, Pastor... No, that's not quite right... but... No, you don't under...." She sighed heavily as the others strained to make sense of the tinny voice coming audibly from handset pressed to her ear. "Yes, Pastor. We'll be here. Yes, in one hour. Both of us." Sali's eyes were bleak as she turned to Sam. "That was Pastor Morris. Mrs. Browning has already got to him... she called from her cell phone in the car. He wants us to talk to him about our 'fall from grace' in one hour. He's coming over."

Sam's chin dropped to his chest as he pondered this latest predicament in his association with the Kelley clan. Marrying didn't strike him with the same horror as it obviously did her, judging by her appalled reaction when the busy body brought up the subject. He raised his head and looked around at the six expectant faces and then to Sali, who had turned her back to him while she stared blankly out the kitchen window.

Sali knew she should be thrilled that her determination to provide her children with Sam Thompson as a father was playing out, albeit through an unexpected route, but she wasn't. She was sure that she had seen stark terror on Sam's face as he denied wanting to marry her. Of course, the whole situation was ridiculous; people in this day and age didn't get married because they had slept together, especially when the sleeping together was as innocent as last night.

Interrupted from her confused thoughts by the feel of a small hand tugging on her t-shirt, Sali looked down to see Jo anxiously peering up at her. "Mama, can I be a flower girl?"

Sam groaned and stood. "I think I'll go see if my house is aired out and get my glasses." Seeing Sali's look of panic he added, "Don't worry, I'll be back before Morris is here. I won't leave you to face him alone."

The house smelled clear of the distinctive odor of natural gas, and the uniformed man walking out the door as Sam approached confirmed that a faulty valve in the water heater had caused the narrowly averted disaster.

After a fast wash in icy water Sam pulled on crisply fresh slacks and a pinstriped shirt. He refused to even think about the coming interview with Pastor Morris, since he couldn't begin to imagine how it might turn out. Idly noticing that he was in need of a haircut he combed his hair, placed his glasses on the bridge of his even nose and drank a glass of water. Then he carefully re-aligned a stack of magazines that had been on an end table but had somehow been knocked to the floor in the ruckus last night, straightened a throw rug, and looked in the refrigerator for nothing in particular. Realizing that he was stalling for time he squared his shoulders and returned to the Kelley household.

Sali had pulled on a cotton sundress and slipped her feet into sandals. There was nothing to be done about her wild mop of hair and she hoped she didn't look as nervous as she felt. The whole situation was completely mortifying.

"Kids, I'd like you all to go outside and play until the pastor leaves. Albert, if you would watch Samuel I would surely appreciate it." Such immediate capitulation would have been suspect if Sali had been thinking clearly but she wasn't so all she felt was relief that Sam and she could conduct the discussion with the cleric in privacy.

Sam knocked briefly and entered. He had enough time to close the door before another knock signaled the arrival of Pastor Morris. Shooting Sali a look that he hoped was encouraging he opened the door.

John Morris was dressed casually in bright new jeans topped by a red-checkered shirt. His thinning hair was damp as though he, too had cut short his usual plans to confront this moral emergency. Face set in stern expression he boomed, "Well, you two. I am very disappointed in the example you are setting for these children."

"Pastor Morris," Sam interrupted. "Please sit down and let's discuss this. I am sure that Mrs. Browning's intentions were good but she obviously misrepresented the situation to you."

"Fine. Fine." Morris chose the flowered chair leaving Sam and Sali to sit awkwardly on the sofa with a good 3 feet of cushion between them. Mockingly, the crumpled blanket they had slept under flagrantly occupied the space. "First let me explain what I understand the situation to be and then you two can tell me why you think the commandments don't apply to you."

Sali had known this wasn't going to be fun but now she

saw that with this one, stupid, innocent episode her standing in the community would be reduced to rubbish. She put her hands over her face and shuddered at the futility of it all.

"Now see there, Sam," Morris intoned. "The poor woman has been wronged and will suffer the consequences of your selfish appetites."

"Oh, this is ridiculous!" Sali blurted out. "We haven't done anything! We couldn't even if we wanted to!"

Sam's head jerked toward her. "Wait a minute! We could do something if we wanted to, if we had half a chance to. We're never alone!"

"You two were alone last night. On that very sofa if I am to understand the circumstances correctly. Isn't that true?"

Considering that the pastor may have missed his calling as a cross-examining attorney Sali covered her face again in horror. Didn't Sam realize he was only making it worse by trying to protect his masculine image with such macho remarks?

Taking a deep breath to calm his rapidly rising pulse, Sam spoke evenly and reasonably. "Yes, we were alone on this sofa last night but I had just been nearly killed from inhalation of gas fumes."

"Did you or did you not spend the night in each other's arms, an unmarried couple in a house of fatherless children, alone in the dark and you, sir," Morris pointed at Sam, "in your underwear when entertaining guests?"

"For God's sake!" Sam stood suddenly.

"I will beg you to not compound the error of your ways by taking the Lord's name in vain!"

"Please," Sali whispered. "Please, can we start over?"

The two men looked at her expectantly.

"Sam and I did nothing wrong last night..."

"Of course you feel that way. And what goes on between

a husband and wife is good in the eyes of the Lord. We just have to rectify the simple trouble of you two not being husband and wife when you started enjoying those good things."

"No, no, you don't understand. Sam and I didn't... I mean, we haven't... That is... Oh, Sam tell him about your accident. Tell him before this gets any worse!" Turning big green eyes toward Sam she noted that his pallor had turned a pasty white.

"I don't know what you are talking about," he said slowly, enunciating each word clearly.

"Well then," Morris proclaimed loudly, "I guess we'll be having a wedding!" At that a cheer was heard from the hallway and the six children burst into the living room, jumping and whooping in glee.

Sali and Sam looked at each other as though they had never seen the other before. Sam saw the soft halo of hair that Sali was forever trying to tame, the simple cotton dress straining across her breasts as she gulped in deep breaths of air, and her fingers nervously plucking at her skirt. He imagined being able to claim her as his wife and these wild beasts as his own children. Sali saw him decisively adjust his glasses, and took in the way his slacks strained over the clean lines of muscle in his thighs and imagined that reaching her goal of giving her children Sam for a father had been accomplished so easily and quickly that perhaps it called for more thought.

Lost in contemplation of the pastor's decision and surrounded by the happy attentions of the Kelley kids, they were oblivious to the fact that Morris had slipped out the door with an uncharacteristically quiet comment about "making arrangements."

Sam muttered something about needing to get away from all the insanity of the past 24 hours and fled to his own house next door. Sali burst into tears and taking

Samuel from Albert she fled to her room where she could cry in privacy. Albert looked around him at his brother and sisters and decided that everyone was crazy.

Sam raked his long fingers through his hair, making it stand on end. Pacing back and forth in the small living room he looked over his options. He could go along with Morris, convincing Sali it would be for the best to marry, or he could tell the pastor to take a flying leap and let Sali weather the censure of her community alone. What he had said to Albert was absolutely true: if he, Sam, wanted to be married there was no woman he would rather have for a wife than Sali, especially now that he believed her incapable of murder, despite what the hulking Hank from the diner said.

Over the past month he had grown to love the kids, looked forward to seeing them, interacting with them and being involved in their lives. Just as he had convinced himself that marrying was the best decision, Sam saw again in his mind's eye, the look of horror on Sali's face when she denied wanting to marry him. And what was that about not "doing anything?" Damn, she *was* Saint Sali! Sam collapsed into a recliner and leaned his head back, eyes closed and asked himself if he could stand to be married to the woman, sleep next to her lush body every night, have the right to hold her hand or stroke her hair and not make love to her? Maybe with time he would be able to reason with her.

Sali lay in bed on her side with a squirming Samuel in her arms, wetting his fat little baby neck with her tears. *How absolutely humiliating.* If Sam went along with the pastor's plans to marry them off, she would have reached her goal but to what end if Sam was unhappy. He was obviously embarrassed about his injuries and lack of ability to perform. She would have to convince him that she didn't want sex, or even like it, but no one must ever know about the farce.

Sali realized she would have to backpedal with Margot because knowing her, one day in the distant future she would come to visit and make some snide or sarcastic remark about Sam's limitations and he would be crushed. So, two lies were necessary to keep peace; Sali would convince Sam she was frigid and she would convince Margot that she was an extremely satisfied woman.

Suddenly she remembered his reaction while she was dragging him from the house the night before. At one point he had thought she was trying to kill him. How could he think such a thing about her and *why*? She was about as peaceful as a person could be, minding her own business, raising her own kids. Even Spencer, in his hysterical, drunken delusions hadn't thought she would kill him. Although, he was fond of saying, "All these bills are killing me."

Sali sat straight up when a horrible thought occurred to her. What if Sam absolutely refused to marry her? How could she face the town or even her kids after this? Sinking back, letting Samuel go to wiggle off the bed, Sali stared straight up at the ceiling. She had to be brave, no matter what. Either way, life wouldn't be perfect, but then what was?

Chapter Nine

Sali's eyes felt gritty and swollen from her crying jag last night. She listlessly poured bowls of cold cereal for the kids, not even commenting when Samuel gleefully threw bits across the room. Even the older kids were quiet, watching their mother drift around the kitchen refilling a glass of milk, wiping up a spill and looking miserable.

"Mama?" Stephanie quietly spoke. The "hmmm?" Sali responded with was as listless as her body language and Stephanie was almost afraid to continue. "Can I go to the library this morning?"

"May I." Sali's correction was automatic but the tone of her voice spoke loudly that she didn't care if Stephanie suddenly started saying "ain't" and wearing striped skirts with polka dotted blouses.

"May I go to the library?" Stephanie corrected herself.

"We'll all go, Mama." Albert looked around the table daring any of his siblings to contradict him. Jo's eyes grew wide and Bridget shrugged as though to say she was up for an adventure.

"Sure. Just be careful and be back in an hour." Going back to mindlessly wiping the kitchen counter Sali was barely aware that the older kids had put their bowls and glasses in the sink and slunk out the door leaving Samuel to throw more cereal at their backs from his high chair.

"What're we goin' to the libary for?" Bridget asked, skipping along beside Stephanie.

"We need a book about weddings. We need to know how to plan one since Mama is acting like she doesn't care."

"Is Sam going to move in with us?" Will asked Albert, confident that his older brother would know the answer.

Albert, trudging along holding Jo's sticky hand in his, pondered that question. "Probably, since we already live there and there are more of us than him. But it will be crowded if he brings his computer and books and records."

"I know! I know!" Bridget yelled, hopping backwards to look at her brothers and sisters. "We could build a hallway from our house to Sam's house!"

"That's dumb," Albert snarled even as he contemplated what sorts of things he could find on trash pick-up day to build a hallway.

The library was housed in a large stone building. In compliance with handicapped access laws there was a new elevator at a back entrance, but the kids liked climbing the wide stairs and pushing open the heavy doors to be assailed with the scent of tons of paper and ink in a whoosh of air. Albert grasped Bridget's shoulder, and leaning down whispered fiercely, "Be quiet in here or else!" She nodded happily as they all followed Stephanie to the computer to look up weddings.

After typing in some keywords and hitting the 'enter' key Stephanie motioned toward an aisle and started in that direction.

"Your mother's a tramp..." a chunky boy whispered as they passed by him. Albert whirled around, eyes narrowed half believing he hadn't heard right.

"What did you say?" he whispered back.

"Your mother is a tramp. I heard my mom say it at dinner last night. She's fooling around with your neighbor." The boy's squinty eyes held malice as he gleefully watched for a reaction

"What do you mean, 'fooling around'?" Bridget asked, remembering to whisper just in time.

"My mom said she's acting like a floozy," the boy countered.

Bridget wasn't sure what any of it meant but she could tell it wasn't good. "You take that back or I'm gonna, I'm gonna... I'll beat you up!" Her voice had risen with each word until at the last she was yelling. To top off her threat, just to show she meant business she pushed the boy with all of her might. Stumbling backwards, arms cart wheeling in the air he crashed into a cart of books sending it rolling down an aisle.

Old Mr. Greene, at the end of the aisle, looking for a book on slug control in the home garden got out of the way in the nick of time by flattening himself against the shelves of books causing a whole row to fall off on the other side.

One aisle over, Emma Albright who was recovering from surgery on her left big toe, the result of a bicycling accident where her foot had gotten caught in the chain and half amputated, screamed as the books came crashing down on the thick bandage bristling with metal pins.

The librarian ran over, took in the sight of Bridget with her fists still raised and chin thrust out like a boxer's, the chunky boy sitting on his chunky bottom halfway down row G, Mr. Greene breathing heavily, still flattened against the teetering shelves of books and through the now empty space between, Emma Albright squatting down examining her toe for signs of serious damage. "Out!" the librarian said quietly. And then pointing with one bony finger in the direction of the big glass doors, she repeated loudly, "Get out!"

The Kelley kids, except for Bridget started toward the door. Albert realized that Bridget wasn't following and grabbed her arm, dragging her toward the exit.

Sam had gone for his walk as usual but decided he wasn't up to any confrontations in the diner. Lacking his usual determined and energetic stride he wandered slowly up and down the narrow streets. Detouring by City Hall he passed the library just as Sali's kids came barreling out. Will was crying, Stephanie's face was brick red and Bridget was struggling against Albert who had a death grip on her arm.

"What is going on?" he called to them at the top of the stairs.

Bridget suddenly started to cry loud, gulping sobs, "A boy in there said Mama is a floozy!"

Sam's mouth dropped open. "What?" The kids had reached the bottom of the steps and now all but Albert were crying. He squatted down and put his arms around the three younger kids as Albert described what had happened moments before.

"This is unbelievable!" Sam groaned. "Don't worry kids. Your mama and I will handle it and it will all work out. Let's go home." Holding out his hands to Jo and Will they trudged down the street in miserable silence.

Samuel pulled himself up on the gate and screeched when he saw the parade of his people coming down the sidewalk. Sali had been sitting on the steps watching the baby play and felt her heart beat faster when she saw that the kids were bringing Sam with them. Afraid she would hyperventilate and pass out she consciously slowed her breathing down but couldn't help laying one trembling hand against her chest.

"Oh, Mama!" Stephanie cried as she came through the

gate, and hurled herself into her mother's arms. The other kids followed leaving Albert and Sam standing a few feet away. Sali looked up from the brown haired heads pressed against her middle and raised her eyebrows in question at Sam.

"We need to talk," Sam said cryptically after the kids had described their encounter with the wild fire spread of rumors. "Can you get a babysitter so we can go out to dinner and discuss this situation?"

A neighbor girl, a teenager with long blond hair and a knapsack full of crafts for her charges, arrived about six that evening after Sali had fed the kids a casserole dinner. Sam had disappeared after bringing the kids home and arranging a time to go out to dinner and no one had seen him since, although Bridget informed the group around the table that his car had been missing for the better part of the day.

Sali put on her dressiest outfit, brushed blusher across her pale cheeks and was just spritzing herself with some coveted perfume when she heard the sound of Albert greeting Sam at the front door.

"Hi," she said quietly, suddenly feeling very nervous. Sam was wearing a suit, his hair freshly cut, and looked as uncomfortable as she felt.

"Shall we go?" At her nod he held the door for her. They walked to his driveway where a new mini van sat, still sporting dealer's stickers.

Sali waiting until Sam had opened her door and helped her in, then seated himself in the driver's seat before trusting her voice. "New car?" Her inner self cringed at the idiotic comment and was gratified that Sam merely nodded.

They drove to a very nice restaurant one town over where Sam hoped they wouldn't see anyone they knew. The silence was becoming nearly unbearable and he was grateful when his request for a secluded spot was honored. The waiter hovered near as they sat down and took Sam's order for a bottle of wine.

Sali was tied up in knots. Sam's expression was so forbidding, barely sparing her a glance. "Sam, what is this all about?" she asked, laying her hands flat upon the ivory tablecloth to still the slight tremble in her fingers.

Reaching across the table Sam wasted no time in getting to the meat of the matter. He took her hands in his. "Sali, will you do me the honor of becoming my wife?"

If Sam had announced that he was really Elvis and shopping at K-Mart, Sali couldn't have been more shocked. "What?" Her mouth dropped open in shock and she had to consciously close it after noticing she was drawing the attention of other diners.

"This whole situation has degraded to the point where the kids are suffering. I know it will blow over eventually, but in the meantime Jo, Will and Bridget are getting a lesson in morality that is not appropriate." Sam looked earnestly at her face.

Sali wrenched her hands from his and clenched them together in her lap. Her emotions see-sawed between outrage and hope. "You want to, *to marry me* because the kids are getting flak from other kids?" she asked in a husky whisper.

"Well, that's part of it, but of course I like you. That is, I like you a lot and we get along well and... Dammit, Sali, we could have a good life together." At the look on her face his hopes plummeted. He had tried and failed even before the wine was served.

"Sam, I don't know what to say. I guess I should ask if you've thought this out. I mean, it's my reputation and my kids who will suffer. Why do you care?"

Rubbing a hand across his jaw he shook his head in

confusion. "I don't know. I guess you and your kids have grown on me. I care about your reputation and your kids and it seems like it would be the right thing to do." Interrupted by the waiter pouring wine, his words hung in the air between them.

As the waiter walked away, Sali took a fortifying sip of the white wine and drew in a deep breath. "Maybe."

Sam's eyes darted up to hers. "Maybe?"

"I guess we should talk about some practical matters. Like, where would we live and... other stuff." She took another sip, this one longer and deeper in hopes of finding courage to approach the subject of sex, or rather that lack of sex.

"Okay. That makes sense. You saw I bought the mini van today. There are enough seat belts for all of us. That's practical. And I put a deposit down on a house today. It's a big house, with six bedrooms and a huge yard."

"Oh, Sam," Sali's voice grew low and soft with emotion to think that he had spent the day arranging things to make their lives better. "That's sweet but you have to be sure about this. Taking on all of my kids is a big undertaking. If I marry you I lose my widow's benefits and can't ever get them back. I have to think of the future."

"That's what I am thinking about! My accident settlement gave me enough money to take care of all of us with the proper management."

"Okay. Yes, the accident..." She licked her lips nervously and looked around the room in panic, anywhere but at him, trying to get up the nerve to talk about the physical side of marriage.

Sam watched Sali's nerves reach the breaking point before he realized what was upsetting her so much. A strong sense of disappointment washed over him to know that sex disturbed her so much that she couldn't even bring herself to talk about it. Maybe dear, old, departed Spencer had been a brute or maybe she had been abused at some other point, but he was sure that Saint Sali had it in her to be a passionate, responsive woman.

Apparently she viewed sex as merely a way to create children and since she knew he couldn't father any through conventional means she didn't want to have anything to do with it.

"Sali," he said calmly, forcing her to look at him. As their eyes met he felt tender compassion toward her and the troubles she had faced. "You're worried about sex, aren't you?"

Sali stopped breathing for so long she thought she would faint. Taking a deep breath she forced herself to look him right in the eyes. "Yes, Sam. I've thought about it and I think I can handle it but I do worry that it will begin to bother me."

"Do you want more children?"

"No! No way!" Her conviction in what she was saying was unmistakable as she emphatically denied wanting to add further to her already over-filled household. "I love them all but enough is enough. Besides, some day I'd like to find out what I want as a woman, not just as a mother. Once Samuel is in school maybe I'll go back to college and get a degree."

"Sex is for more than just children, Sali. Does that bother you? I mean, because of my accident?" Sam had lowered his voice to an intimate level.

"That's what I'm talking about. I don't want more kids and I think I could handle it but then I wonder..." She felt her face grow hot with a deep blush and she looked away in consternation.

"I promise you, I'll make every effort to accommodate your wishes." He held out his hand and after a moment she put hers there on the hard warm surface of his palm and somehow it seemed like a pledge. Somehow, Sam swore to himself, he would either reunite her with her sexual nature or deal with platonically sleeping next to her night after night. "For the kids' sake I think we should share a bedroom, though. We want them to believe our marriage is as normal as any." Wondering how he would survive the torture of cold showers he lightly squeezed her fingers.

"Okay. If that's what you want." Sali figured it would stretch her endurance to the breaking point but maybe it would become easier with time. The gaze Sam leveled on her was so piercing she felt the need to change the subject. "Tell me about the house," she asked and there followed a description of the large family home he had noticed on his walks and had, only this day put a deposit on.

On the way home, on impulse, Sam drove past the sturdy old building, stopping the van at the curb so Sali could catch a glimpse. "We'll come back tomorrow so you can see the inside. There's an old claw foot bathtub in the master bath that I know you'll love." He grinned at Sali and she flushed, imagining herself naked, chin deep in bubbles only steps away from him in their marriage bed. Seeing the blush across her smooth cheeks his grin faded and he leaned toward her. "Trust me, Sali. I won't hurt you," he murmured as his lips brushed hers in the lightest of caresses. He felt, rather than heard her sigh and quickly sat up and put the car in gear. Berating himself for already being tempted by her, they drove home in uneasy silence.

As soon as Sali entered the quiet house the babysitter relayed a message from Pastor Morris who had dropped by while Sali and Sam were at dinner. "He said to tell you that the wedding is scheduled for day after tomorrow at the church and that unless he hears otherwise it will be just himself and Mrs. Browning who has agreed to act as witness. I didn't know that you and Mr. Thompson were getting married so soon. The kids told me you were engaged but even they didn't know it would be Friday. Boy, they were sure excited! I had a hard time talking them into going to bed."

Sali groaned. This was all happening too fast and she needed time to think about it all. Wanting to be alone she offered to stand in her open front door and watch the young woman walk to her house across the street and down a few doors. The girl took the hint and gathered her things leaving Sali to her thoughts but as she reached her door she paused and turned back to call out loud enough for Sali to hear her across the street, "Oh, I forgot! Pastor Morris also said to remind you to get the marriage license."

There was a lot to be done in a short period of time and Sam was determined to create a list rather than think about the decision he had made to marry Sali, but try as he might his mind kept wandering back, paper and pen forgotten in his hand.

Considering himself a logical, intelligent man he was flabbergasted to discover that he had no real reason for wanting to marry the woman. Of course any caring person would want to spare a widow and her six children the sort of gossip that was surely, even now, spreading like wild fire through the small town but to sacrifice his own bachelor status to make that happen was a whole other issue.

Why, he asked himself, was he excited and anticipating their life together with pleasure? Was it all about the kids, because he did love them and he believed that they loved him. It sure wasn't about sex; Sali was about as uptight on that subject as a person could get. Maybe it was merely companionship although, he had to admit, he hadn't ever noticed feeling unduly lonely before moving next door to the Kelley family. Now, if he didn't know what was going on in their house, didn't see them and hear a story or two, didn't catch a glimpse of Sali hanging laundry at midnight, he felt left out.

The sound of the gate next-door squeaking open and slapping shut caught his attention. The babysitter going home, he supposed. Then he heard the sound of her voice call out, surprisingly loud in the quiet dark of the evening, "Oh, I forgot! Pastor Morris also said to remind you to get the marriage license."

Sam put pen to paper for the first item on his to do list.... "license"

Next door, Sali curled up in bed in her cotton night-gown and thought about the events of the evening. She knew why she wanted to marry Sam: for her kids. They loved him and he was so good with them. A mother was supposed to sacrifice herself for her kids, wasn't she? But why didn't she feel like she was being sacrificed? She would be a good wife to him, even if it meant killing that side of herself that was a woman and needed a man. She would be affectionate and loving and supportive in the face of his disabilities.

But, for just one moment, she was going to imagine what it could be like if he had all his equipment. For just tonight, she allowed herself to fantasize about a complete relationship with him that included the physical side of love.

"Love?" Sali sat straight up in bed. Where did that word come from? Reaching for her pad and pencil on the night stand next to the bed she began a list of things to do over the next two days to keep from even mentally wandering down a path that was sure to break her heart.

"License - wedding on Friday." Because the thought of Bertha Browning being rewarded for her meddling ways by being the witness, Sali wrote, "Call Margot to come for wedding." And then, before she could forget, she picked up the phone and dialed.

Thursday dawned bright and clear. Sali had spent an hour on the phone with Margot the night before and then was too keyed up to sleep until she finally fell into a doze over her list at about 3:00 am. Consequently, she woke to the pressure of a small finger on her eyelid and Bridget's distinctive whisper, "She is too asleep!"

Sali opened her eyes and saw Bridget's face about two inches away from her own. "Good morning," she muttered sleepily.

"You need a wedding dress, Mama!"

"Pastor Morris said you're getting married tomorrow!"

"Can I call Mr. Tom Son 'Daddy'?"

Sali sat up and took Samuel from Albert's arms, pulling him onto her blanketed lap. The kids looked so happy, excited even, that she hadn't the heart to discourage them by not getting into the spirit of the wedding. "You girls can help me pick a dress from those I already own. We can fancy it up somehow. Albert, you can give me away. I didn't even think about calling Grandma and Grandpa to come and now there isn't time. I called Aunt Margot, though, and she's driving here from Las Vegas. She'll be here this afternoon."

The kids all jointly sighed in relief. Sometimes Mama could be difficult and contrary citing adult reasons that they "wouldn't understand."

Breakfast was a happy affair with pancakes and hash browns. Samuel didn't know what was going on but he knew that everyone was smiling so he banged his spoon on the tray of high chair and made a few experimental sounds.

Suddenly, there was Sam, standing in the back doorway, smiling at the scene that met his eyes. "I knocked but

I guess it blended into the baby's banging."

Sali looked at him shyly, as the kids gathered around. "Would you like some breakfast?"

No, thanks. I'm getting ready for my walk." Sam stumbled backwards as Bridget barreled into his arms, hugging him with an intensity that he had never felt before.

"Can I call you Daddy after you and Mama get married?"

Not wanting to step on any toes he looked at Sali. She shrugged. "Well, Bridget," he said carefully, "I would be honored if you would call me Daddy but I never, ever want you to forget your first father." Bridget sighed and hugged him tighter.

"Dada!" Samuel looked as shocked as everyone else when the word came out of his mouth.

In the confusion of the chatter of children's voices as they tried to entice the baby into repeating the word, Sam walked over to Sali where she leaned against the counter, cradling a cup of coffee in her hands. "How did you sleep last night?"

"Okay. I made a list of things to do. Pastor Morris came over while we were out..."

"Yes, I heard," he remarked cryptically. Sali raised her eyebrows in question. "I heard the babysitter call out to you that we were supposed to get the license today."

"Oh, God! If you heard her inside your house that means everyone else on the street did too." Sali put one hand over her mouth as she considered the implications of this newest form of spreading gossip. Just holler it out on the street.

"They're all going to know soon enough, Sali. Anyway, I thought maybe we could go over to the house after I get back from my walk. I want to make sure you like it before I finalize the deal. Since it's empty we ought to be able to move in as soon as the papers are signed."

Sali agreed, touched that he was considering her opinion, and they exchanged items on their respective lists, finding that, for the most part, they were identical. Sam left for his walk, the girls went to search Sali's closet for a suitable wedding dress, and Albert wandered off under the backyard elm to think serious thoughts about being the man of the family in this one last duty; giving his mother to Sam. After tomorrow the weight of responsibility would fall off his shoulders.

Sali looked out the kitchen window at her young son, slim shoulders looking less fragile, now that the weight of a misplaced responsibility was being lifted off him.

On the last leg of his walk, Sam entered the diner as usual, knowing that Hank, and possibly others would be aware of the upcoming nuptials as well as the events leading up to this moment. He was not disappointed. As he stepped in the door every head turned his way. As he walked to the counter numerous, hearty congratulations accompanied by manly slaps on the back followed his progress.

"Glad to know those rumors about you weren't true," Hank commented as Sam sat down on his stool.

"Since there are so many rumors flying I'm not sure which ones you mean," Sam replied with a smile. "Can you be more specific?"

Hank looked just a mite uncomfortable and shifted his hefty weight slightly on the stool. "About your accident over to the factory. All us guys heard you'd been, um, emasculated. So's when I heard you were the one sleeping over at Spencer's, uh, I mean, Sali's, I figured everything was in working order, so to speak."

Sam stood up and looked at Hank in horror, "What?" His eyes traveled the diner and he could tell from the embarrassed looks, and quickly turned heads that this rumor was common knowledge. They all, every last person in the diner, thought that he was missing his private parts. Realizing his reaction was at least as interesting as the subject matter he sat back down. Struggling to control his voice he pitched it just low enough and just loud enough for others to hear. "Well, like you said, that was a rumor and thanks to your mother-in-law it's been proven wrong."

The next half-hour spent drinking his coffee was the longest of Sam's life. He was anxious to get Sali alone and find out if this "emasculation" rumor was the cause of her discomfort about sex. Could it be, he asked himself, that he had been wrong all along; that Sali was making do with a bad situation, and trying to protect his feelings by holding back sexually? Not that they'd had much opportunity to explore that side of their relationship, but he mentally went over their conversation at dinner last night, wondering if he had misunderstood what she was saying.

Chapter Ten

Sam showered under the brisk spray, closing his eyes into the stinging needles of water. Mentally he wandered over the tasks he had to complete today. Instead of feeling overwhelmed he was invigorated by the challenge. He was marrying Sali, and obtaining six interesting children in the bargain. Last but not least, was the hope that Sali's reluctance to enter into the sexual side of their relationship was based on a stupid rumor. He vowed to get her alone for a serious talk at some point today so that the little misunderstanding could be cleared up. He chuckled into the steam billowing around him. He couldn't wait to see her face!

"Mr. Tom Son," a voice called out from another part of the house. Sam turned the water off to the shower and called out, "just a sec!"

Toweling dry quickly, he pulled jeans on and padded out into the living room still sporting a towel slung over his shoulders. Bridget stood looking at the sleeves of old LPs in a glass-fronted case in the living room. "Look, I can read!" Bridget's face screwed up into intense concentration as she sounded out the letters on an album cover. "Elllv…isss!"

Sam smiled indulgently. "Yep, you're right. That's Elvis the Pelvis."

"Elvis the Pelvis?" Bridget dissolved into helpless giggles. "Elvis the Pelvis!" she shrieked. "What's a pelvis?" she asked.

"Um," Sam floundered. "It's your hips," he said swiveling his hips in a controlled imitation of Elvis Presley's famous moves. Bridgets giggles became even louder as she attempted the same hip movements.

Cringing, Sam tried to change the subject, "what did you want, Bridget?"

"Mama wants to talk to you. Elvis the Pelvis!" Her tongue rolled the syllables around like the finest wine. Bursting into giggles once more she ran out the door sing-songing the singer's less-than-classy nickname.

Sam dressed in tan slacks, topped with a crisp white shirt. Forgoing a tie he left the top button undone and slipped his feet into loafers sans socks. He picked up his list of things to do and then walked next door, considering that it was a miracle the kids hadn't worn a groove in the sidewalk with their frequent comings and goings between the two houses. Soon they would all be together in the big house and the load of worries that Sali had been operating under would be gone. Whistling he approached her door but stopped short when he heard the voices coming from inside.

In the babble he could make out Sali's protests. "Girls, I can't wear that to get married in!"

"But Mama, it's pretty!"

"It's way too short. And way too red. And way too wild. I don't even know why I still have it!"

Sam grinned as he tried to imagine Sali in a dress that was "way too" short, red and wild. Maybe he could talk her into a private fashion show. First, though, he would have to explain to her the misunderstanding about the extent of his injuries.

His quick rap on the front door went unnoticed in the hubbub so he pushed the door slightly and let it swing open. The scene inside was classic Kelley; several dresses were draped across the sofa. Stephanie was holding up a red silky, spaghetti-strapped cocktail dress while Jo leaned against Sali's knee where she sat in the flowered chair. Meanwhile, Bridget was gyrating her hips chanting, "Elvis the Pelvis." Try as he might, he couldn't control the mirth that threatened to overtake him. Finally, giving in, he laughed until tears ran from his eyes, shocking the four females into a stunned silence.

Sali recovered first. "Well, I'm glad to see you find this amusing!" She rose and grabbed the red dress from Stephanie's hands.

"I'm sorry," he began, holding up his hands in supplication before another outburst overcame him and Jo began laughing along with him. Knowing that the child had no clue what was so funny made Sali laugh along with them. The sound of their hysteria, interspersed with Bridget's voice trilling her new favorite phrase brought the boys running into the room, Albert carrying Samuel. Soon, they all were laughing until they collapsed onto the furniture and floor like puppies after a hard run. In the ensuing quiet Sam looked around him at the people he had chosen to be his family. Catching Sali's eye he tried to send her the message that he was happy and would make her and her children happy.

Sali rubbed her aching cheeks and looked up at Sam. She felt mesmerized by his eyes and then grew flustered. It took all of her will power to pull her gaze away while she stood and began gathering up the dresses the girls had brought out from her closet. "I couldn't get the babysitter today. She had already promised the day to another family."

"That's okay. We can all go."

The van was just big enough to hold the kids and car seat. It took a few moments before the kids had each checked out the windows, built-in drink holders and fold up arm rests and were actually belted in. Sam patiently waited until Sali nodded at him that he could start the motor.

Sam pulled up to the big house on Hill Street and turned off the car. The kids were, for once, shocked into silence as they stared at the balconied building.

"It's a palace." Bridget whispered.

"It's a mansion." Stephanie countered.

"If you all like it, it's ours." Sam smiled as they struggled to quickly extricate themselves from the seat belts and clamber out of the van. Running helter skelter up the bumpy walkway they left Sali and Sam carrying Samuel to follow.

The front door opened in a whoosh of cool air scented with the odors of old house, wood, dust and history. The kids hung back on the wide covered porch letting Sam go first and then stepped inside reverently, looking about them in awe. A foyer opened to a large living room on the right and a small office on the left, which Sam said would be perfect for his computer equipment. On the far side of the living room, an arched opening showed a square dining room large enough for a table for 12. Beyond that lay the kitchen, with tall glass-fronted cupboards, long tiled counters and a space in the center for the old oak table.

As they trooped through the rooms Sali's head spun. This was like something she had only dreamed. After having seen five bedrooms and two bathrooms Sam finally led the way to the master bedroom. An open, spacious room, it opened onto the upstairs balcony. Two attic closets on either side of the French doors had plenty of space under the sloping room to stash treasures like baby books and hand made mother's day gifts.

The bathroom was small by modern standards, but cozy, dominated as it was by a large claw-footed bathtub. A mullioned window looked out over the side yard where huge elms held court, providing shade for a grassy area below. Sali leaned her forehead against the cool glass and imagined actually living in this house, bathing in that tub, sleeping with Sam in the room behind her. Dimly aware that the kids had run off to pick and choose which bedrooms they wanted, Sali was unaware of Sam's presence until she felt his hand on her shoulder.

"I was hoping I'd get a chance to talk to you alone today." Sam figured Samuel didn't count since he wouldn't understand the conversation.

Sali turned her head slightly and could see his wavering reflection in an old full length mirror on the wall. Baby Samuel straddled one hip and was carefully picking at the button on Sam's collar.

"I was in the diner this morning and Mrs. Browning's son-in-law Hank..."

"I remember Hank. He was a friend of Spencer's." Sali turned full around and looked at Sam straight on.

"...yes, well. Hank mentioned something interesting. About my accident. And my injuries." He paused, considering how to go on but lost the opportunity for privacy when the kids came barreling back in, crowding around the adults in the bathroom. At Sali's questioning raised eyebrows, Sam mouthed "later" and turned his attention to Albert who wanted adult confirmation that as the oldest he should get first pick of the bedrooms.

The next stop was the Real Estate agent's office,

where Sam finalized the purchase of the house. The court-house was within walking distance so they set out as a happy parade down the street. Bridget was the first to dis-cover that the cavernous open stairwell of the huge, old building made a great echo chamber. "Elvis the Pelvis," she called out, first in a normal voice, then in a low growling voice and then in a high falsetto. Sam and Sali exchanged a look that seemed to say, "should we be as mortified as we feel? Nah." They shrugged and after consulting the Build-ing Directory followed a maze of hallways to the Clerk's office.

Standing in a row against the high counter, the chil-dren watched quietly while Sam and Sali filled out the proper papers and left with a license to be married neatly stowed in Sali's crocheted string bag that was slung over her shoulder. Right before Sam pushed the heavy doors open to leave the building, Stephanie surprised even her-self by emitting a high pitched squeal that echoed satisfac-torily and brought a small smile to her usually quiet lips.

Lunch consisted of grilled cheese sandwiches and tomato soup. Just as the meal was finishing up the sound of a car door slamming sent Sali to the front window. "Margot!" she screamed. Suddenly Sali and a tall, red-haired woman were hugging each other in the open door-way, laughing and leaning back to look the other up and down then hugging and laughing all over again. The kids gathered around watching while Sam hung back.

"Oh, gosh, where are my manners?" Sali laughed with a hand to her heart. "Sam, this is my good friend Margot Hamer. Margot, this is Sam."

Stepping forward Sam held out his hand and grasped Margot's before he realized that she was going to try to bring him to his knees with a death grip. Pulling him for-ward by his hand she wrapped her other arm around his shoulders in what appeared to be a hug, but was in fact, a stronghold. Pressing her mouth to his ear she fiercely whispered, "You had better be good to her or I'll choke the life out of you!" Abruptly letting go of him, Margot watched as he staggered back, a look of shock across his features. It always paid to make people think you were just a bit around the bend, Margot told herself.

Sam felt a little in the way and unnecessary once Margot started hauling bags and boxes in from her partially restored Karmen Ghia. Sali shook her head in amazement. "It's like Mary Poppin's bag! How did you fit all of that in there?" Margot laughed as she struggled to extricate one last bag from the furthest reaches of the area behind the seats.

"I think I'll just go home and try to get some work done," Sam remarked but no one paid him the least attention so he went out the back door, hopped the fence and went home.

"Oh, I'll admit he's good looking but if the man can't put out..." Margot poured another glass of wine for Sali as they sat cross-legged on her bed after the kids were all asleep.

"Margot! Sex isn't everything. He bought us a beautiful house and a van and he's great with the kids." Sali fiddled with her wineglass and plucked at the quilt she sat upon.

"Come on! That's all fine and dandy but are you sure you can forego sex for the rest of your life? Who knows what sort of weird psychological trip he's on because of getting mutilated. I think it's a mistake, Sali. I'm sure he's very kind and very generous but if you can't share yourselves with each other in a way that's complete and total, what do you have? A sugar daddy?" Margot jumped up and leaning in close to the dresser mirror began smoothing her eyebrows with one crimson-tipped finger.

Sali took a gulp of wine and shook her head. "We talked about it the other night and I told him that I have my concerns with the sex issue. He said he'd make an effort to accommodate me. I didn't ask for the details of his injury but maybe there's something he can strap on or pump up that will make it possible."

"Oh my God!" Margot groaned falling backwards onto the bed. "That's gross! I can't believe you even said it!"

"No, it's not gross. I think I can love Sam and I think he can love me because we both love the kids and want what's best for them. I think it's sweet that he wants to satisfy me and if you're going to be disgusting about it you can just forget about talking about this anymore." Sali put her hands over her face.

"Ah, I'm sorry, Sali. I won't tease you anymore. Anything you two can do to make yourselves happy is great with me. I just want you to be happy, finally. Now, let's change the subject. Look at the dresses I brought and see if one will work better for a wedding gown than those old disco dresses you had moldering in the back of your closet."

Sali was up before anyone else in her house on Friday morning. She made herself a cup of coffee and sat on the back steps to watch the sunrise. There was just a hint of fall in the air at that early hour, which always made her feel a little melancholy. After at least an hour's debate last night Margot and Sali had agreed on a dress for the wedding. They had polished off the wine and eaten an entire bag of chips making it necessary to take the quilt outside and shake off the crumbs before they could go to sleep. Now, here she was up way too early, on her wedding day. Thinking herself a fool for feeling nervous, she decided she had better concern herself with making breakfast since it may be the only substantial meal any of them would get until evening. But for one more moment she would stand here in her own back yard, breathe deep of the fall breeze and enjoy her solitude.

Sam stood at the kitchen window in loose drawstring pajama bottoms that hung low around his slim hips. Sipping a cup of coffee he stared blankly out at the lightening day. As the dawn developed he realized that Sali was standing in her back yard, wearing a gauzy white nightgown. Though her head was tilted back with her face to the sky like a wild animal sniffing the air for danger, something about the attitude of her body made him think she was sad. Her hand came up and swept across one cheek and he realized that his intuition was correct; she was wiping tears away.

Without thinking about it beforehand Sam opened his back door and silently padded outside. Vaulting the picket fence, he was behind Sali in an instant but when he put his hand on her arm she jumped, spilling her coffee.

"Oh, I didn't hear you come up!"

"I saw you out here and thought you looked sad. You're not having second thoughts, are you?"

"No, are you." She braved a look at him from the corner of her eye and was relieved when he shook his head.

"No, I've never been more sure of anything. Besides, I can't imagine living in that big house all by myself." He wrapped one arm around her shoulders and drew her to his side. "What's making you sad, Sali?" he asked gently.

"I'm just being silly. It's the smell of autumn in the air and the kids will be going back to school soon..." her voice broke, "...and I'll never stand under this elm tree in my nightgown at dawn again." A sob broke from her throat and turning she buried her face in Sam's neck.

Somehow Sam knew instinctively that Sali didn't need words, just a strong shoulder to cry on. He pulled her

156 ~ IRENE LAFETRA

around to him so that he could hug her properly and let her cry it out.

After a few moments Sali pulled away and, running a shaky hand through her tangled hair she took a sip of her cooling coffee. Looking at Sam from the corner of her eye, she watched as he looked up at the big elm and took a deep breath of the cool dawn air. His drawstring pants exposed a concave belly and his smooth chest was a study in clean, defined muscle. He obviously hadn't combed his hair or shaved yet this morning and she noticed the dark shadow across his jaw beneath tousled, thick dark hair. A foreign feeling of heat and fluttery sensation gathered in her lower belly and it took a moment for her to recognize it as the beginnings of physical attraction. With a sinking feeling she wondered how she would manage to contain her needs when every pore of his body seemed to set her off.

Sam caught Sali looking at him, and when he turned his head to her gaze he held her eyes with his. In the shadowy dawn his sight was reduced to an intuitive vision and he sensed rather than saw the passion she was carefully holding in check. He felt his own desires rise and considered that if he didn't reign himself in his pajama bottoms would tell the story of his fully functional state before he could broach the subject tactfully.

The back door opened marginally and a dim spear of light spilled out across the lawn. "Mama?"

"Out here, Stephanie," Sali called to the thin girl wearing a shorty nightgown in the open doorway. Turning to Sam she whispered, "Will you come over for breakfast? Or do you want to enjoy your own last moments of solitude?"

Stroking her cheek with the back of one hand his voice was rough as he whispered back, "Sometimes solitude just feels like loneliness."

"Why are you really marrying me?"

"Because… I can't help myself." At that enigmatic reply, Sam turned and vaulted the fence back to his own yard leaving Sali to wonder what in the world he had meant.

Margot made hash browns, scrambled eggs and stacks of pancakes, keeping the excited children occupied while Sali soaked in the tub. Using the full array of her bath pretties, carefully protected in their miniature steamer trunk, she luxuriated in steamy, fragrant bubbles. By the time she stepped onto the fluffy rug next to the tub her stomach was fluttery with nervous butterflies and she had a twitch in one eyelid.

Between Margot and Albert the kids all got bathed, dressed and set up with coloring books on the living room floor while Sali dressed and Margot took a quick shower. Sali had just sat down to begin applying makeup when her red-haired friend poked her head around the door. "I don't know how you've done it all these years, Sali. The kids are great but they are a full time job. I was wrong to judge you for marrying Sam. He's nice, he's financially stable, he's good with the kids and if you don't get to play doctor with him he will more than make up for the lack in other areas."

Sali held very still and wondered at the things Margot said. Needing a second set of hands had never even crossed her mind; she was so used to taking care of the kids by herself it never occurred to her that Sam's presence might actually help her to get more accomplished. But, she wondered, what more did she actually want to do? She had been so busy, her time filled with so many necessary activities for so long, that her mind went blank when she tried to think of something she might want to do, as opposed to all of the many things she had to do. Maybe Sam would think she was stupid and boring. All she was, was a mother. Soon to be a wife. She knew how to do those things but Spencer had thought her boring and dull which had ultimately led to their mutual unhappiness. Shaking her head to clear the confusing thoughts, she leaned closer to the mirror and began brushing mascara onto her already long lashes.

At exactly ten minutes to ten Sam knocked on the front door. Margot greeted him, surrounded by pink-cheeked, neatly dressed children. At the sound of his voice Sali came out of her bedroom at the exact moment Sam looked up. He forgot to breathe while he took in the sight of her in a calf-length, swirly dress of emerald silk shot through with a subtle pattern woven into the fabric. Her hair, for once, was allowed free reign and curled in wild abandon about her shoulders, making a soft dark cloud to offset pearl earrings and glowing cheeks that had more to do with nerves than makeup. "You look lovely," he spoke quietly making Sali's cheeks grow pinker still.

"Are we ready?" Margot asked the group at large and was answered with a childish roar of enthusiasm from the eager children.

Pastor Morris met the group at the front door of the parsonage with a hearty hello and large gesture of his arm. Sweeping them inside he led them to his dusty, crowded study where his tiny birdlike wife waited. Sali was relieved that Mrs. Browning had, for once, listened to what she was told and not shown up. Behind the large wooden desk where the Pastor was carefully filling out paperwork, a picture window overlooked a green oasis of a garden. Shrubs, glistening grass, a tiny rock lined fish pond and stalks of tall flowers drew Sali's attention. She glanced at Sam and saw that he had been looking at the same scene. He raised his eyebrows in question and Sali nodded imperceptibly, marveling that he could read her mind.

"Morris, would you mind performing the ceremony in your garden? It's beautiful and Sali and I both enjoy nature." Sam was trying to be diplomatic, without having to come right out and say that the study was a disaster and he didn't want to have a conversation in it, much less get married there. Morris looked startled at the request but agreed readily so they all followed Mrs. Morris as she led them through an old fashioned kitchen and out into the woodsy back yard.

Morris cleared his throat as he opened up a small bible. Sali felt tremors run through her body and suddenly Sam reached out and took her hand, gently squeezing her fingers while Jo leaned against her legs and watched the proceedings in fascination. Margot held onto the squirming Samuel and the other children clustered around.

"Dearly beloved," Morris began. As the familiar words were spoken the kids became a little restless, and Sam surprised them all by suddenly producing a handful of jelly beans from a jacket pocket and passing them out to the over-excited children. Sali squeezed his hand in thanks for his foresight.

Suddenly it was over. They were married. There was a moment of stunned silence before Sam lightly kissed Sali's lips and the kids cheered. After a wedding luncheon that was actually a picnic in the park they went back to their houses, changed clothes, packed bags and Sam whisked Sali away in the van leaving Margot in charge of the kids with Albert's expert guidance.

"You know, I didn't expect a honeymoon," Sali said as soon as they were on the freeway heading north.

"We both need a break and some time to ourselves. We'll have fun. I booked us a room at the lodge at Lake Tahoe. It's a long drive so you ought to relax and get some rest." Sam expertly steered the van along the Interstate highway, and though Sali was determined to stay awake and be company for him, she fell asleep almost immediately.

Waking drowsily as they pulled up under the covered valet entrance, Sali gathered her purse and stepped out into the chilly mountain twilight. The scent of pine and damp earth surrounded her and she took great breaths in an effort to calm her jittery nerves.

The room was large and overlooked a forested area that led down to the huge alpine lake. Sali held onto her elbows as she stood looking out at the last light fade from the surface of the water, surreptitiously watching Sam's reflection in the window as he moved around the room. Approaching her from behind she watched his arms reach out around her and so wasn't startled at his embrace.

"Sali, we have to talk about some things," he began. His hands caressed her lightly just beneath her breasts. Feeling the tremors running through her body, he stilled his hands and rested his forehead on the top of her head. Breathing deeply of the scent of her clean, soft hair, he sighed. "But it can wait. Neither one of us ate much at lunch and I, for one, am starving. There's a restaurant overlooking the lake. Are you up to a short walk?"

He knew he was being a coward, putting off the inevitable but suddenly he felt unsure. What if he had been wrong and she really didn't like sex? What if, instead of being thrilled that their marriage would be complete in every sense of the word, she was horrified to find out she would not, after all, be spared the horrors of her marital duties? Shaking his head lightly he led the way across the road and down a path to the very edge of Lake Tahoe and a quaint timbered restaurant.

The meal had been romantic and delicious. They talked about the children, inevitably and then as their thoughts meandered mellowly they spoke of favorite music and the merits of compost. The walk back was slow because of the steepness of the incline, and Sam kept his arm around Sali's shoulder to warm her against the cold mountain air. After a moment of silence they fell back into their comfortable companionship and chatted about the stock market, alpine lakes in general and what furniture they would need to buy for the new house.

Sali took a quick shower and nervously drew her plain cotton nightgown over her head. Coming out into the large, luxurious room she saw that Sam had the gas fireplace going and the music channel on the TV playing soft forties music. He smiled encouragingly at her while he grabbed his pajama bottoms and entered the bathroom for his own shower.

The drumming of the water seemed to echo in his head as he considered how he could bring up the subject of sex. Not ordinarily a nervous person he found himself extraordinarily preoccupied with trying to divine the future. What if she was appalled that he expected a sexual relationship with his wife? What if, after all this he couldn't do it? It had been a long time. Was this performance anxiety?

Letting the water stream over his shoulders and back, he tried to get a grip on himself. Looking down at the part of himself in question hanging in a state of complete relaxation, he tried to will it to rise. When no answering response was forthcoming he put his hands over his face.

He was making himself into a nervous wreck about the whole thing. He'd never had a problem before and he wouldn't now and it was all just a huge, stupid misunderstanding. Sali would be glad. He had to believe that and hold onto that thought. Sali would be glad but he still took his time drying his hair, shaving, brushing his teeth and pulling on the pajamas before finally entered the bedroom once again.

Sali was curled on her side breathing deeply and evenly. Her lashes fanned over her cheeks and her rosy lips were slightly parted. Both hands, held together as though in prayer, were under her cheek. Sam stood looking down at her and grinned wryly. So much for performance anxiety, he said to himself as he pulled back the covers and crawled in next to the soft, lush body of his sleeping wife.

Sali felt the hand cupping her breast before she was even entirely awake. The sensation, so foreign, yet so good, had worked its way into her dream. As she struggled up from the downy cocoon of sleep and sank down into the drugging lethargy of desire she became aware of a warm body pressed against the length of her back. Just as her mind registered that this was Sam and they were married he pulled her to her back and his lips found hers. Shock gave way to a mindless thrill as his tongue parted her lips and seeking, found hers beginning a parody of the passion that her body craved.

Resignation that this would go nowhere, but unable to stop what would surely amount to torture, Sali's hands crept up to Sam's neck and she pulled him tighter. His mouth left hers, trailing kisses down her neck and to the edge of her simple cotton nightgown. It was too dark to see his face but she sensed he was looking at her questioningly. Wordlessly she sat up and drew the shift over head, tossing it to the floor and he resumed his exploration.

When his hot mouth found one tightly budded nipple she gasped in pleasure and arched her back. Mindlessly, allowing what must be for him, an act of charity, Sali was powerless to stop him from pleasuring her body. His hands roamed slowly and surely across her heated skin, pausing to explore the places where she unmistakably found greater pleasure. She ran her hands down the length of his sides, wanting to touch him, give him equal joy, but unsure what his reaction would be if her explorations were too intimate. Instead, she gave herself up to his ministrations until she felt caught in a vortex of desire, Gasping his name she clutched his shoulders. Barely aware that he had moved over her and between her parted thighs, her gasp became a shocked cry when the unmistakable sensation of being joined with her husband found it's way through her foggy, passion drugged mind.

Sam groaned as he entered her, burying his face in the crook of her neck, as she wrapped her legs around his hard, muscled buttocks. Her hands gripped his shoulders as she drew him nearer, deeper, trying to absorb him into her very soul. In a flash of insight, Sam knew that this was where he belonged, and what they were experiencing, this melting together was the belonging he had craved his whole life. Even though they wouldn't create children together, they were creating a new entity, a new life in the joining of their psyches and spirits. Almost immediately he felt her find her release and within a few moments he joined her.

"Sam, I thought..." she paused, trying to think how to word it without insulting him.

He raised up on one arm and looked down into her face warmly glowing in the light of the fire. Swollen lips, eyes still glazed with passion spent, and wondered how he ever could have thought she was frigid. "I know what you thought. And someday, I might tell you what I thought." Before she even had a chance to wonder what he meant his mouth claimed hers once more and they were lost in the discovery of each other.

Postscript

Sali quickly and expertly dished up the holey eggs to the five bright faces around the big oak table. Sam retrieved a fallen fork, grabbed plastic tumblers from the glass-fronted cupboards and poured orange juice, all while listening to Bridget tell about a dream she'd had in vivid, excruciating detail. He caught Sali's eye and winked. "Where is Albert?" she asked the group at large.

"It's trash day," Sam answered and they all sighed in unison, knowing what that meant. Albert was the king of scavengers and was, no doubt, out gathering "stuff" to use in his inventions. Just then the bell on the front gate jangled, an attempt to keep them notified when Samuel tried to escape the confines of his own yard, and Bridget jumped up and ran to the front door. Since Samuel was safely ensconced in his highchair, frantically stuffing his cheeks full of holey eggs they all looked up expectantly. Bridget's excited conversation and subsequent headlong flight back into the house with a bundle of letters, along with John the Mailman's hearty "so long" as the gate bell jangled again, told them that the mail had arrived. Bridget had proclaimed herself the family deliverer of mail and carefully handed out the letters, advertising and magazines.

Sali shook her head in wonder at the antics of her middle daughter. Taking her cup of coffee she stood in the open back doorway and watched Albert enter the yard from the side with the garden wagon holding the base of a kitchen blender, the handle of a weed eater, and what appeared to be an old movie projector. He went directly to the shed at the back of the property where he began going through his find. "Don't forget it's a school day!" Sali called to him. Sam's arms snaked around her from behind and pulling her firmly against his body she felt the evidence of his attraction to her. Chuckling to herself she marveled that she could have missed the existence of his full functionality for as long as she had.

"Have I told you lately that I love you?" he whispered in her ear.

"Only about a hundred times a day. But that's okay, because I love to hear it almost as much as I love to say it. I love you back, Sam Thompson."

Suddenly, bursting around them and through the doorway, the children came, calling to Albert, laughing and shouting and Sali thought, I wonder how I managed before Sam.